Dog Gone

Dog Gone

A Paws and Pose Mystery

Shannon Esposito

Misterio press

* * * * *

Visit Shannon Esposito's official website at
www.murderinparadise.com

* * * * *

Cover Art by Dar Albert

Formatting by Debora Lewis
deboraklewis@yahoo.com

* * * * *

ISBN-13: 978-1-947287-05-1

ONE

The only thing that makes Christmas feel like Christmas in Florida—considering the balmy, seventy-degree weather in December—are the decorations. Fortunately on Moon Key—a private Gulf coast island for the insanely rich—that was covered. And by covered I mean the whole over-indulgent island would soon be covered in twinkling lights, glittering fake spray snow, giant wreaths, gold poinsettias and palm trees wrapped up like candy canes in red velvet ribbons.

Today was the first Saturday in December. It was the day Christmas decorating elves would descend upon Moon Key mansions, beach bungalows, condos, golf courses, and the country club. In other words, the decorating madness would begin.

"Rich people are crazy," my friend, Lulu, mumbled, as we gathered our day's shopping bags from the trunk of my vintage—aka old and moldy—VW Beetle. It was a gorgeous, low-humidity day, and I'd hoped a little Christmas shopping would improve Lulu's mood, but now she just seemed depressed and tired. She'd been down in the dumps for weeks. I offered her the only thing I could, a nod of concession. She had every reason in the world to believe that, after the trauma she'd just suffered at the hands of her millionaire, psycho-ex-boyfriend.

"Nope, I've got that one." I took the oversized bag from her and pointed to her rounded belly beneath the pink, fuzzy sweater. "The doctor said no heavy lifting."

"You're worse than my mother. And that's not an easy thing to be." She sighed, grabbing the lightest bag and hanging it off of her pinky finger while smirking at me. "Happy?"

"Very." A smirk was in the same family as a smile, at least.

I led the way to the front door, through a group of Santa's elves working hard and fast to add my boyfriend, Devon's, beach bungalow to their finished list. One said elf—actually, a well-built man in a green uniform and elf ears—was squatting while hooking up an extension cord to a strand of lights he'd wrapped around the Bird of Paradise plants. I frowned at the decorated tropical plant. It was like throwing a cowboy hat on a city gal in a business suit. It just looked wrong.

He glanced up as we approached and his gaze snagged on Lulu. I watched in amusement as his expression morphed from surprise to pleasure. This was the typical reaction she got from men because of her flawless brown skin, large gold-green eyes, corkscrew curls and thousand-watt smile.

I glanced at her to see if she'd noticed. She had, though I saw her expression shift as she quickly raised her guard. I imagined her hastily adding a crocodile-filled mote to the fortress around her heart, along with various other slathering beasts waiting to tear into any man who dared to try to get close.

The guy stood up slowly, adjusted one crooked elf-ear and held out his hand to her. "Leo. Leo Gold. And you are?"

Lulu's green eyes narrowed as her body stiffened. "Pregnant."

Poor Leo. He opened his mouth but nothing came out. "I..." His hands spread helplessly. "Congratulations?"

With a noise of disgust, Lulu rolled her eyes and reached for the door handle.

"Here, let me get that for you." Leo rushed in, trying to salvage the situation.

She turned on him like a poked cougar. "I'm pregnant, not helpless."

He held up his hands in surrender, his eyes still sparkling with interest. "Got it."

I shook my head and, after she stormed inside, I whispered, "It's not personal, Leo. She's just gone through a really traumatic experience."

He was still staring at the doorway. His blue eyes were wide, like he'd just been hit in the face with an infatuation stick. "She's incredible."

Now it was my turn to throw my hands up. Who knew getting blown off by a pregnant woman could be such a turn on. I would never understand men. "Nice ears, by the way."

Our two dogs, Buddha—my mostly white, seventy-pound bulldog-mix—and Petey—Devon's brown mutt with white paws—already had their noses shoved in the shopping bags we'd piled beside the naked nine-foot fir tree in the living room.

I breathed in its scent deeply. "Mmmmm." It was one of my favorite smells in the world, fresh cut Christmas tree. Of course, it couldn't be too fresh, not with all the needles it was shedding, but it was worth the mess.

"Get your head out of there," I chastised an over-enthusiastic Petey, as he ripped open one of the bags. "And stop drinking that water." I nudged Buddha's face out of the Christmas tree's water.

Lulu lowered herself to sit cross-legged on the Mexican tile floor and then got busy unboxing shiny red and gold bulbs.

Clearing my throat, I decided to test the waters. "So the elf, he seemed nice... and handsome and interested. Had that younger Elvis vibe going on." I refrained from saying Elf-is, instead just chuckled quietly at my private joke. "You know, when he still had sparkling eyes and swiveling hips."

Lulu's pale green eyes glittered at me beneath dark lashes. "Don't even go there, Elle. I'm never getting involved with another man. Ever." She rested a hand on her protruding belly. "It's just me and this baby now, we don't need anyone else."

"Okay. But you know you and the baby are not really alone. You have me and Devon, and Hope and Beth Anne and Violet. We're all here for you."

Buddha and Petey had finished inspecting the packages and moved on to properly greeting the humans. I fended off their slobbery kisses with ear scratches.

Lulu raised her head and looked at me full on with watery eyes. Her small shoulders slumped. With a sigh, she reached over and squeezed my hand. "I know and I do appreciate your friendship and support. It's the rest of my life I'm not sure how to deal with. Like having to close The Gumbo Pot because of Selene's lawsuit. I feel so lost without my restaurant, without being able to cook for people. I don't even know who I am right now."

I forced an encouraging smile. "I know it's hard, but you'll find your way."

I still couldn't believe Selene was trying to take Lulu's restaurant. Lulu had made a one-time error in judgment and slept with Selene's husband, Michael, which resulted in the baby she was now carrying. Since Michael had given Lulu the money to open The Gumbo Pot years ago, Selene now wanted it back. Not that she needed the money. She mostly wanted Lulu to be as miserable as she was, after losing both her husband and her son.

"Besides it's only temporary," I said, trying to stay positive. "We'll find some way to save your restaurant, I promise."

"Maybe. Maybe someone will drop a million dollars in my lap for Christmas." Glancing toward the door, and then letting her gaze fall to the gold ornament in her hand, she asked, "So what's the deal with the Christmas elf out there anyway? Devon doesn't decorate his own place?"

I suppressed a grin. This was a good sign. She hadn't closed the door on her heart forever. She just needed some time to heal. "Nope. He's actually not allowed to."

She glanced up. "Not allowed? Like banned? What'd he do? Put up really ugly decorations last year?"

"No." I laughed, unboxing a second set of red and gold ornaments. "It's not just him, it's everyone. The homeowner's association here has very strict decorating rules. There's only one company, Gold Holiday Lights, that's allowed to decorate Moon Key, and everyone has to have uniform decorations, no colored lights, only one animated figure, stuff like that."

She raised an eyebrow. "And what if someone goes all rebel and God forbid hangs up colored lights?"

I pushed a wave of long, auburn hair out of my face. "They'll get fined like a thousand dollars a day until they take them down."

Lulu was staring at me as if I'd lost my mind. Maybe I had because I suddenly felt the need to defend this decision. "It's really because of the holiday parade boat show. It has to look good from the water, and that means coordinating decorations for the overall appearance of the island, not just individual houses. They do a big dancing lights show to music so it has to be synchronized over the whole island."

She shook her head and snorted. "Wait, Gold Holiday Lights? Didn't that... elf person outside say his last name was Gold?"

I thought about it. "Yeah, he did, Leo Gold. He must be part of the family. You know who else is part of the family? The HOA President, Eva Gold. I've never met her, just heard horror stories about her temper, but apparently her brother owns Gold Holiday Lights."

"Well, that is a much better explanation for their island decoration monopoly than looking good for the little people in their boats." She stroked Petey's brown head, which was now planted firmly in her lap beneath the baby bulge, his doey eyes staring up at her with contentment.

I wanted to tell her she was just being cynical, but she was probably right. If there was one thing I was learning, it was that it's all about who you know in the world of uber-money. I believed the word was *nepotism*.

She hung a gold ball dusted with silver glitter on the tree beside her. "So, have you decided on Devon's Christmas present yet?"

I frowned. "Nope." I had no idea what I was going to get him. What do you get a millionaire who can buy himself whatever he wants? What I wanted for him more than anything in the world was for his parents' murderers to be put behind bars. That's the reason he'd given up his photography career, moved here to Moon Key and become a private investigator in the first place. To find out exactly what had happened the night his parents died and who was responsible.

Changing the subject, I pointed at her belly. "I think it's time to feed that baby lunch and I don't mean you, Petey. We've got some leftover veggie pizza Devon made last night." I pushed the box of decorations I was working on underneath the tree. "I'll warm some up for us."

As I stood up, my cell phone rang. I fished it out of my bag on the way to the kitchen. It was probably Devon checking in from his secret trip to Georgia. When I'd dropped him off at the airport yesterday, he still wouldn't tell me what he was doing. He said it was a surprise, but promised it was nothing dangerous. It probably had something to do with investigating his parents' murders, even though he swore it didn't.

I checked the number. Nope, not Devon. "Hello?"

As I opened the fridge, a soft female voice said, "Elle Pressley?"

Not a voice I recognized. "Yes?" I pulled the tin foil off the plate of cold pizza.

"Hi, this is Talia Hill. I was told you do private doga lessons, and I was wondering if you were available to come to my house tonight."

I froze. Then walked back around the counter and lowered myself onto the bar stool. I was staring at Lulu, who was staring back at me, but I wasn't really seeing her. Mostly I was trying to process what was happening right now.

"Miss Pressley? Are you still there?"

I clutched the phone tighter so I wouldn't drop it. "Yes. I'm here."

"Would nine o'clock be good for you?"

"Yes. Of course. Whatever you need. I can be there. Nine o'clock." I smashed my lips closed before I rambled on more.

Silence, except for the sound of my heart pounding in my ears, and then she asked, "Do you need my address?"

"No... I... I know where you are... live. Don't worry, I'm not a stalker."

Did that sound creepy?

"Okay." She chuckled softly. "See you then. Thanks."

She hung up. I stared at my phone. "Thank you."

"Elle?" Lulu was now standing in front of me, her eyes wide with worry. "What's wrong? Is it Devon? Did something happen?"

"Ha!" A burst of half-laughter, half-goose honking escaped my lungs, startling both of us. I grabbed my chest like I could stop my racing heart from the outside. "Oh my goddess in heaven, Lulu! Do you know who that was? That was Talia Hill! She wants me to come to her house tonight for a private doga lesson. Me! I'm going to pass out." I leaned over and put my head between my knees.

"What! You're joking!"

When I looked up, Lulu was shaking her head in disbelief, setting her shoulder-length spiral curls in motion. "*The* Talia Hill?"

Sitting upright slowly, I felt my mouth stretch into a huge grin. Lulu covered her own mouth with her hands, and we screamed like two school girls.

TWO

Talia Hill! Did I know which mansion was hers? Of course I did. Everyone did. She was a celebrity among celebrities, a star above every other. The most celebrated actress of our time. A recluse who came to Moon Key at different times of the year but barely gave anyone a glimpse of herself.

There was a rumor at the Pampered Pup Resort and Spa, where I taught doga (doggie-yoga) classes, that she'd arrived for Christmas early this year, but no one had spotted her yet. Rita Howell, the manager at Pampered Pup, kept us all on high alert, making sure the facilities were spotless in case she decided to bring her dog in, and reminding everyone to treat her like a person and not pester her for an autograph. She was a huge fan. I imagine she'd break her own rule, if Talia ever did show up there, and be the first one in her face with a pen and paper. Or maybe she'd just have her sign her arm and then get it permanently tattooed. Like I said, big fan.

I glanced at Buddha strapped in the seat beside me. His eyes were half-closed. I'm sure he was wondering why I was dragging him out during the time he and Petey were usually taking their pre-bedtime nap.

I sighed at his indifference. "Do you know where we're going? We're going to meet Talia Hill!" I still couldn't believe it. *Breathe, Elle. Don't act like a freak.* I checked my neck in the mirror for hives. So far, so good. "Okay, some ground rules, Buddha. No peeing on her bushes. No eating her décor or slobbering on her furniture or chasing her cat if she has one." She seemed like she could have a cat, too. "And please stop Mommy if I blather on like this in front of her."

I took three deep breaths. One wasn't going to cut it.

Get a grip, Elle. She's a person, just like you.

No, no she's not.

I shook my head and felt my pulse rise. She's a goddess. A legend. She probably eats light and air for breakfast. She probably wakes up in the morning with her hair and makeup perfectly in place, with birds singing at her window in celebration that she's in the world.

Her Christmas lights were partially up. While they did turn her mansion into a miniature version of the Disney castle, that wasn't why I stopped the Jeep abruptly in front of the driveway.

"Whoa, look at that, Buddha."

At the sound of his name, Buddha glanced at me.

"No, out there." I pointed and we stared up at the enormous glass figure of a terrier sitting with a happy grin, all lit up with twinkling blue and white lights from the inside. It had a red satin collar with a giant gold nametag that said "Holly."

"Holy puppy. That thing must be what... eight feet tall? Definitely not HOA approved." I grinned. I liked this woman already.

With my yoga bag slung over my shoulder, my heart flinging itself against my chest and Buddha panting at my side, I walked up the driveway. The queen-of-the-silver-screen's part-time home was a professionally landscaped, two-story Mediterranean U-shaped mansion, with at least five visible rod-iron balconies.

As I climbed the semicircle marble steps, I spotted the place where the decorating elves had stopped for the night. I knocked on the iron and etched-glass door lightly at first, then a bit harder. It opened and a petite, almost transparent woman stood there in flannel pajamas, mascara smeared beneath her eyes.

Did I have the wrong mansion? Was this really Talia Hill, silver-screen goddess?

I gaped at her, stunned by how different—and tiny— she was compared to her commanding screen presence. If I breathed too hard on this woman, she'd blow away like silvery ash. Also, she looked like someone had just crushed her world. Her blue eyes held the sorrow of a million break-ups. Did something just happen?

A knot of anxiety began to form in my stomach and wind its way around my lungs. "Is this a bad time?"

She peered around my shoulder as if she were expecting someone else and then her demeanor instantly shifted. Her face lit up and she shook her head. "Sorry. Elle, right?"

I was so confused by the sudden change all I could do was stand there like my feet were nailed to her front porch. I managed a nod.

"You're fine. I was just practicing my lines for a new film, and it's hard for me to get out of character. Thanks for coming on such short notice and so late." She reached out and scratched Buddha under the ear. "Hello, big guy. Well, come on in you two."

"This is Buddha," I said, still feeling off-balance. I stepped inside, resting my hand on Buddha's head for emotional stability.

Closing the door, she led us through the foyer—complete with marble pillars and a ginormous glass chandelier looming above us—and into the grand room. It was decorated with simple elegance—white sheer curtains, multiple vases of pink roses, birch wood furniture with light blue accents. Very zen.

"When I'm not filming, I usually stay up at night and sleep in the daytime, much more peaceful. Ginger's in here." She slid gracefully onto the sofa and patted the cushion beside her. "I thought we could get to know each other for a minute before we begin the lesson. I've just had Marcel make us some of his famous hot chocolate." A silver tray sat on the table with two steaming, white mugs. "Apparently the secret is to melt seventy-percent dark chocolate with some coconut oil."

As I took a seat, I refrained from pinching myself to see if I was dreaming. I kept Buddha on his leash, but he was straining to greet Talia's West Highland white terrier, Ginger, who was curled up in her dog bed, just the twitch of her pointy ears acknowledging our presence. She didn't seem ready to greet us.

"Buddha, sit." His brown eyes rolled up to meet mine, and then he plopped down with a sigh, making sure he had a good view of Ginger.

I adjusted myself on the sofa to angle toward Talia. "I think my dog is smitten."

Talia's laugh was light as a feather, too. "She is a beauty, isn't she? She's been through a lot recently, and she's very hormonal. She's just come out of being in heat, so I wanted to do something special for her."

I heard a catch in her voice and wondered if I should ask what was wrong. Or was whatever happened too painful to talk about? I didn't need to worry, though, because Talia stood and went over to the fireplace mantle, retrieving a silver-framed photo that sat next to an ornate silver earn.

Returning to the sofa, she handed it to me. "This is Ginger with her sister, Holly. We lost Holly to cancer four months ago. She was only six years old."

"Oh, I'm so sorry. They are gorgeous." I stared at the two Westies sitting side by side in front of a lake, their long white coats backlit by the sun. Then I remembered the large glass dog out front. "So your glass dog outside, that's a tribute to her? To Holly?"

"Yes." A small shiver ran through her body and she stiffened before getting up and returning the photo to the mantle. "Holly and Ginger, they were born on Christmas day, so the holiday has always been special to me. I wanted to do something grand for her, to let her know she would never be forgotten. Do you like it?"

I swallowed a swig of the creamy melted chocolate and nodded. "It's really beautiful. I can't believe you got the HOA to approve it."

She waved a petite hand. "Oh, they didn't. In fact, I was confronted by a charming little southern woman with a surprising mean streak, who told me I'd be paying a thousand dollar fine for every day it's up." Her blue eyes sparkled with mischief.

"Yeah, that pesky rule." I shook my head. "You'd think they'd see a beautiful memorial like that and realize it would only add to the Christmas spirit on the island."

I felt Buddha shift and glanced down. Ginger had decided to come greet us, and Buddha started sniffing her with uncharacteristic excitement.

"Easy big guy." I made him sit back down so Ginger could sniff him without getting stepped on, since she was half his size.

Her shiny black button eyes flicked from Buddha to me. She held a squeaky frog in her mouth.

"Hello, pretty girl," I said soothingly. She seemed wary of me so I didn't reach to pet her yet. After a minute, she relaxed and sat in front me, leaning against my leg. Then, looking up, she gently laid the squeaky frog in my lap. "Oh, you want to play?"

I heard the small catch in Talia's throat, but it was too late. I had picked up the frog and chucked it across the room. It landed by the fireplace with a squeak of protest.

Ginger didn't run to fetch it. Nope, instead she stared at me with her ears tilted forward and her jaw shut tight, those shiny eyes now looking at me in utter horror.

My heart dropped into my stomach like a stone. "Oh God, she doesn't like to fetch?"

"I'm sorry, Elle. I should've warned you," Talia said over her shoulder, as she hurried to retrieve the toy I'd just tossed across the room.

I was mortified that I'd just played fetch with a movie star.

Ginger didn't take her eyes off of me until Talia returned with the frog and held it out to her in cupped hands. Finally, with one last look of bewilderment aimed at me, Ginger took the frog back, holding it gently in her jaws and giving a little whine.

I watched in confused silence as the dog climbed back up in her bed, dropped the frog into a pile of squeaky toys and nosed them toward her belly.

Talia laughed softly as she placed a warm hand on my arm. "I'm sorry. Don't feel bad. She's going through a false pregnancy. She was showing off her puppy to you. It's her favorite."

I winced. "Her puppy?" Oh heavens. I'd just chucked her puppy across the room. "She's going to hate me for life."

"She won't." Talia gifted me with her radiant smile, and I felt a measured bit of relief.

"I'm so sorry," I said.

"Well," Talia said, shaking her head, "let's see if we can't get her mind off of those... puppies for a bit."

"We can only try." I unrolled my yoga mat in front of the pink one Talia had already placed by the fireplace.

"Come on, girl," Talia called, patting the mat.

Ginger slunk over reluctantly, the green frog held gingerly in her jaws. She eyed me suspiciously as she positioned herself between Talia's feet.

I couldn't blame her. I unsnapped Buddha's leash. He lay down and stretched out his front paws until they were touching Talia's mat, his attention resting fully on Ginger, who was staring at him, her head tilted.

I shook my head. "Definitely smitten." I scratched the brown spot above his tail. "Ready to earn your keep, Buddha?"

He responded by stretching further towards Ginger, his jowls now resting on the edge of Talia's mat.

Talia giggled and scratched his ear. "I've met guys like you. Hopeless romantics, the most dangerous kind."

I cycled through a few rounds of stretches for both us and the dogs and then a bit of massage to try to relax Ginger. About fifteen minutes into the lesson, a skinny, short man dressed in jeans and an orange, floral Hawaiian shirt bounced into the room.

Ginger wagged her tail and proceeded to hop off the mat, cross the room and drop the frog at his sandaled feet.

"Oh, look at the precious baby." He scooped up the slobbery squeaky toy. "She's beautiful, Ginger." He scratched under her chin and glanced up at us with an amused smile. "Sorry to interrupt. Did you want me to take Ginger for her nine-thirty walk or wait until you ladies are finished?"

"Sure, you can take her." Talia pushed herself off the mat. "I don't think we're succeeding in getting her mind off of her puppies anyway."

I hated to admit defeat, but she was right. Ginger was anxious to get back to nursing her nest of squeaky toys. And Buddha wasn't helping with his infatuation. I rolled up my mat.

Talia turned to me. "Sorry, I should've asked. You don't mind if we cut the lesson short this time?"

I slid my rolled up mat back into its bag and pushed a stray wave of hair out of my face. "Not at all. We can try again after her false pregnancy is over."

"Great. She's all yours, Diggs. Maybe you can get rid of some of her anxious energy."

"Your wish is my command." He dropped a kiss on the dog's head. "Come on, Princess."

Ginger followed him happily to the door, her short legs scurrying to keep up, baby frog still held gently in her jaws.

"I don't know what I'd do without that man," Talia sighed. "It's hard to find someone I would trust with my girl." A shadow of something dark, anger or grief maybe, crossed over her pale features. She shook it off. "Anyway, I feel bad that I had you come over for nothing, Elle. I'll still pay you, of course." She returned to the sofa. "At least come and finish your hot chocolate. It actually tastes better as it cools, if you can imagine that. Besides, I don't get much time to just sit and chat with someone who's not in the business." She smiled at Buddha as we followed suit. "Especially someone who understands that dogs are family, not property."

I smiled. "That's the nice thing about Moon Key. Most people here believe that."

An awkward silence made me start fidgeting with my cup. My confidence on the mat didn't translate to the sofa, especially when I remembered who I was sitting with.

Say something, Elle.

"So, I loved your last film, Jar of Hearts. You and Matt Sterling have such amazing chemistry."

She grunted in amusement. "You want to know a secret? The man is barely five-foot-six. He wears two-inch platform shoes."

I stopped mid-sip. "No way!"

She nodded. "Yep. That's why I get cast as the leading lady in his movies, too. Being five-foot-two, I put the "tall" in his tall, dark and handsome. My ex-husband was so jealous of Matt. He used to insist on being on set during love scenes, which made everyone uncomfortable. Except Matt... I think he actually enjoyed riling him up. Little did I know my ex was projecting because he'd actually been cheating on me. Hence the ex part."

"I'm sorry," I offered. Of course, I knew about the drama already, as it had played out for months in the media. It had been a bitter divorce. Why anyone would cheat on Talia Hill, I would never understand. She was beautiful, talented, rich and sweet as far as I could tell. What more could a man want?

She waved it off. "It's fine. I've got ninety-nine problems but a man's not one of them." He eyes shone brighter, like she'd been lit up from the inside as she added, "I've got my Ginger and that's all I need."

Just then Buddha lifted his head, his ears erect. He pushed himself off the floor and scrambled across the wide expanse of tile toward the front door, a low growl lodged in his throat.

Talia and I shared a worried glance.

"Does he do that often?" she asked, her hand fluttering to her throat.

"Not without a reason," I whispered. "Expecting anyone?"

She shook her head.

Buddha let out a sharp bark that made us both jump up and hurry to the door.

Talia peered out. "I don't see anyone."

"You don't have a stalker, do you?" I reached down and rested a hand on Buddha to quiet him. The fur on his back was standing straight up. That was really out of character for him. Sweat broke out on the back of my neck.

"Yes, a few, but no one's ever been able to get to me here on Moon Key. That's one of the reasons I come here. I feel safe." She crossed her arms and her pale features pinked. "No one is going to take that from me. I won't live in fear here." She slipped into a pair of gold backless sandals.

"Hang on. We'll go with you." I grabbed Buddha's leash and dug my cell phone out of my bag. "Okay, boy, let's go see what's got you worked up."

Buddha scrambled out the door. It was all I could do to hang on to the leash as he bolted down the marble stairs and out into the circle driveway, letting out a frantic bark that I'd never heard from him before.

The hair on my arms prickled as he pulled us toward the road. Despite the slight chill in the air, sweat rolled down my sides. An answering bark sounded somewhere in the distance. Talia's breath was coming in short gasps beside me. The night was too quiet. No frogs. No bugs. No night birds. Something was definitely wrong. As we crossed the end of her driveway through the open black iron gates, what that something was hit us like a lightning bolt.

"Diggs!" Talia screamed.

THREE

"Oh my God." We rushed over as close as we could get to the man lying sprawled in the wreckage of shattered glass and Christmas lights that used to be the statue of Holly.

I held Buddha close to me so he wouldn't step in the glass. He was still straining to sniff the area frantically. "What happened?"

Talia had her hands pressed to her chest. In the flimsy gold sandals, she carefully picked her way through the glass-strewn grass and dark strands of lights. "I'm coming Diggs. Oh God. Oh God."

"Talia, be careful!" I cried out. "I'm going to call security and an ambulance." Holding onto a straining Buddha with one hand, I dialed security.

Diggs wasn't moving or speaking. Hopefully he was just unconscious. "We need help at Talia Hill's place. Call an ambulance. Please hurry!"

Pocketing my phone, I called to Talia, who was now sobbing into her hands beside Diggs. "Help is on the way." But, by her demeanor I could tell it was too late. Diggs was gone. My heart dropped. "I'm so sorry," I whispered.

Buddha and I stood quietly, giving Talia a moment to grieve in peace. It seemed so wrong... a man losing his life to a backdrop of twinkling Christmas lights.

She suddenly jumped to her feet. "No!" Her long hair escaped its ponytail and swirled around her shoulders as she turned in quick, frantic circles. "Oh God... Ginger!" she screamed. "Ginger!"

Two golf carts rounded the corner, their headlights glinting off the remains of the glass statue. In the bright light, I caught a glimpse of the blood soaking through Diggs's hair and streaking his face.

I turned away as Talia picked her way back towards me, sobbing. "Elle, you have to help me find Ginger."

"Of course. She couldn't have gone far. We'll find her," I managed, though my own voice was thick with panic. "She probably just got scared and is hiding somewhere."

Talia nodded and chewed at her thumbnail. Even in the soft glow of the surrounding Christmas lights I could see the shock dilating her pupils.

Four Moon Key security guards hopped out of the golf carts. Two of them picked their way through the scattered glass toward Diggs and the other two approached us. One of them, unfortunately, was the head of security, Alex Harwick. *Perfect.* Alex was a forty-something ex-football player, and typical good ol' Florida boy, who didn't understand or accept rejection. I'd stopped counting the number of times he'd asked me out since I'd started working on Moon Key.

Right now he was walking toward me with his hand up in greeting. "Elle." Then, smoothing his dirty-blond hair down self-consciously, he stared at Talia and cleared his throat. "Miss Hill."

Talia turned to him briefly, but her eyes were darting around the area. "We have to find Ginger," she moaned through her grief.

"Ginger?" Alex asked, glancing back and forth between us.

"Yes, Ginger. My dog." She turned on him. "She's a white terrier, about twenty pounds. Diggs was walking her. Now Diggs is there," she motioned behind her without looking, "and Ginger is nowhere." Her hands flew to her mouth as her body began to shake uncontrollably. "Diggs is dead. This can't be happening."

Her grief was just as commanding in real life as on the screen. I realized her vulnerability was the one thing she didn't have to portray through acting.

Alex peered over at his men. I turned in time to see the one beside Diggs shake his head. Alex pulled out his phone and called the Clearwater police.

⁓❦⁓

"So what's she like? Talia Hill."

I glanced over at Detective Salma Vargas, surprised by her question. She seemed a more no-nonsense type of woman who wouldn't care about celebrities. We were canvasing the area with flashlights, looking for Ginger, while her partner, Detective Farnsworth, took Talia's statement inside and the ME's team dealt with the body.

"She's... nice. Not at all uppity like you'd think she'd be." Buddha had pulled me over to sniff a row of bushes. I shined the flashlight beneath them. "Human, just like us."

Salma made a snorting noise. "Hollywood royalty are not just like us. They live in a whole other universe."

"Ginger! Here girl!" I called softly. The night was so quiet and there was a crisp, clean bite to air. "That may be true, but I do know that this dog is her whole world. We have to find her or she's going to be *devastated* Hollywood royalty."

"I pictured her as more of a cat person." Salma stopped walking and sighed. "All right listen, we've been out here for nearly an hour. The dog is probably just freaked out and hiding somewhere. There's nowhere for her to go, unless she's got a ferry pass. I suggest we call it a night, and you help put together a search party for her in the morning, when you can actually see more than five feet in front of you."

I had to agree. The Christmas lights were helping, but not enough as the mansions sat too far back from the road, and there was too much cloud cover for moonlight. All the frustration and sadness of the evening suddenly hit me. My bones felt like lead. "You're right. This isn't getting us anywhere." I sighed. "You have to be the one to tell her though."

Talia took the news as well as can be expected for a person already in the throes of grief and shock. Her eyes shimmered, sending a fresh path of tears down her pale face.

That's when I noticed what she was clutching in her hands. I froze. She saw my attention on it, and a small sob escaped her throat. I let myself fall onto the sofa beside her.

We both stared at the squeaky green frog. Talia shook her head. "She'd never abandon her frog willingly."

My gaze rose to meet the two detectives, who were obviously getting ready to head out. "Something's happened to Ginger," I said. "She didn't just run away."

The detectives shared a glance and then Salma nodded at Detective Farnsworth. "Go on and check the progress outside and finish the neighbor interviews, I've got it." She lowered herself into a corner of the overstuffed loveseat and took out her notepad. "So, Miss Hill, what do you think happened to Ginger?"

Talia pressed her perfectly sculpted nose into a Kleenex and then straightened her spine.

How is it possible that she looks even more beautiful with a red nose and swollen eyes?

"Well, I don't know. I just know that she wouldn't abandon this frog. She went through a false pregnancy and thinks it's her puppy. She must be so distraught, wherever she is." A deep tremor shook her body.

Detective Salma Vargas eyed the squeaky frog skeptically. "False pregnancy?"

"Yes. It's a hormonal condition that mimics a real pregnancy. She even went through a false labor and is lactating."

Detective Vargas shook her head slightly. "I see. Okay, is there anyone you can think of who would benefit from taking your dog?"

"Well, yes, my ex-husband. We had a long custody battle over both the dogs. I won custody, but he would take Ginger in a heartbeat if he could. We lost her sister, Holly, a few months back to cancer."

Salma scratched something on her notepad and then glanced up. "I'm sorry for your loss. That would be Sammy Salazar, the UFC champion fighter? Your ex?"

She wiped her nose with a tissue. "He's retired now but yes."

"Do you feel he's capable of getting violent to get the dog back? Maybe took him from your dog nanny forcefully? Maybe he didn't mean to kill Mr. Diggs but just take the dog." She squinted her eyes, thinking out loud. "Maybe there was an altercation and Mr. Diggs fell into the glass statue, breaking it and cutting himself on the glass?"

One petite shoulder rose. "He has a temper, sure, but I've never seen him physically hurt someone out of the ring."

Salma tilted her head. "Do you know the whereabouts of Mr. Salazar?"

Talia's face hardened, her eyes blazed. "Making an honest woman out of his mistress?"

Salma's mouth curved sympathetically and she shifted her feet. "Anyone else you can think of?"

Talia bit her bottom lip. She squeezed the Kleenex in her fist. Her shoulders slumped and then she looked up and seemed to steel herself again. "No. Well, I mean, my neighbor Nell hated my dogs. She blamed them for the death of one of her peacocks and swore she'd get revenge. And she does seem strong enough to push Diggs into the statue in an altercation. He isn't..." the word caught in her throat. "He wasn't a big guy."

Salma scratched that down in her notebook. "Anyone else?"

Talia blushed and her eyes dropped. "Not that I can think of."

She studied Talia for a moment and then slowly closed her notebook. "Well, if you can think of anyone else, give us a call. We can't do our job if we don't have all the facts."

A fleeting look of guilt crossed Talia's face. "I understand."

"Also, if you have next of kin information for Mr. Diggs, we'll need to notify his family."

"Oh." Talia cringed. "Right. I think he had a sister in North Carolina, but they weren't close."

"All right. We'll check his phone contacts."

As Salma rose, Detective Farnsworth came ambling back in. His mousy hair was in dire need of a cut and his button-down shirt was straining against his belly. His expression was dark and disturbed.

"We have a problem." His gaze flicked from Talia to Detective Vargas.

Detective Vargas rested her hands on her hips. "Other than a dead man and a missing dog?"

"Afraid so." He moved closer and whispered something in her ear.

Her jaw muscles twitched. She turned to us. "The ME has found a wound on the side of the victim's head that suggests our theory is wrong. This may have been an intentional homicide."

"Homicide?" Talia shook her head vehemently. "No, that can't be true. Diggs was the sweetest, most caring person in the world. Everyone loved him. Who would want to kill him?"

Salma rubbed the space between her eyebrows. "I guess that is the million dollar question."

FOUR

The next morning Devon and I headed to the clubhouse with Lulu and my best friend, Hope. Talia had given me a photo of Ginger so we'd printed out "lost dog" flyers. The clubhouse bulletin board was the only place people were allowed to put up announcements or posters on Moon Key, otherwise we'd be plastering them on the side of every palm tree and golf cart around.

Next we headed to Talia's mansion. A cold front had arrived late in the night, and it was a foggy morning, dull and gray and chilly. I zipped up my white cotton hoodie.

"She really had a dog-nanny? That's a thing?" Devon said as he drove, his words a bit slurred from lack of sleep. Neither one of us had gotten much sleep last night. He'd come home late from his secret trip and then we'd stayed up longer talking about what had happened to Diggs and Ginger.

I rolled my head in his direction with a smirk. "Yep. And don't get any ideas, rich boy."

"Wouldn't dream of it." He chuckled. "And you think someone forcefully took the dog because of a squeaky rubber frog left behind?"

"Yes."

At his skeptical glance, Lulu chimed in from the back seat. "Believe me, pregnancy gives you all kinds of new fierce protectiveness, whether your babies are real or not."

He nodded in concession and took a deep drink of the black coffee in his insulated cup. "So, if it was a homicide we find the dog, we find the killer."

My eyebrows rose. "We?"

He rested a warm hand on my knee and squeezed. "If I know you at all, Elle, you've already gotten attached to this woman and her dog and won't rest until they're reunited."

I started to deny it but then sighed. "True but I'm only going to help her find Ginger. We are not getting involved in solving another murder."

Hope snorted from the back seat. "We'll see about that."

I chose to ignore her.

Devon shrugged. "Like I said, find the dog, find the killer."

I pulled my jacket tighter around my neck. "Let's hope not."

Devon parked in front of Talia's iron gates, even though they were wide open, and hopped out of the Jeep. We all climbed out behind him and moved closer to the area the police had taped off.

"It'd been a beautiful glass statue of her late dog, Holly," I said.

"A shame." Devon stepped over the tape and walked around the circumference of glass, which now glittering as the early morning sun burned through the fog. Only the bottom feet remained intact. He bent down and scooped up a handful of the glass, examining it. "This looks like safety glass by the way it shattered into small, round bits." He dumped the glass back on the ground and stood up, hands on his hips.

"Should he be touching that?" Lulu asked.

"Probably not." Studying the look on his face, I asked, "What're you thinking?"

Devon's gaze moved to the remaining feet of the statue. "If a person fell into a statue made of glass this thick, I don't believe it'd actually shatter. Crack maybe. Break off in an area that was weak. But shatter? A falling body doesn't seem like enough force to cause this kind of damage."

I had to forcefully stop the image of Diggs lying there that night from materializing in my head. "Maybe whoever hit Diggs swung and missed the first time, hitting the statue," I offered.

Devon stepped back over the tape. "Maybe. That doesn't really tell us anything, though."

"Except the killer has bad aim." Lulu absentmindedly rubbed her baby bump under her red, cable knit sweater.

"Or bad eyesight." Hope's hands were tucked into the pockets of her brown leather Michael Kors trenchcoat and the tip of her nose was pink from the cold.

I tilted my head in thought. "It was dark out. Anyway, this isn't getting us anywhere and it's cold out here. Let's go talk to Talia."

This time we were greeted by a tall, gray-haired man with drooping cheeks like a basset hound. Despite his appearance, he cheerily invited us in.

"Miss Hill will be down in a moment. She's asked me to get you situated and offer you a beverage. Coffee, tea... fresh orange juice?"

As we entered the greatroom, my attention caught on Ginger's abandoned bed with all her colorful squeaky toys piled up. A wave of sadness hit me. "Coffee would be great. Thank you." I forced a smile. "Marcel, isn't it?"

He returned a nod. "Yes, ma'am."

I swallowed the lump in my throat. "Fantastic hot chocolate you made for us last night." It was the only thing I wanted to remember about last night.

"Thank you, ma'am. And for you all?"

"Coffee," Devon answered. "Black, please."

"I'll have the same," Hope said, slipping out of her coat.

"Water, thanks," Lulu said, taking in the house with a star-struck expression. "I can't believe we're standing in Talia Hill's house."

"Elle!" Talia rushed down the stairs in a black cotton dress and sunglasses that swallowed her face. Her moon-colored hair flowed loose down her back. She hugged me like we'd been lifelong friends, her small fingers surprisingly strong as she gripped my arms. "Thank you for coming back. Did you get the flyer up?"

"Yes, we did." I motioned behind her. "Devon and I put it up before we came here. He's a local private investigator and he'd like to offer his time. All of us would, in any way we can to find Ginger. These are our friends, Lulu and Hope."

Talia slid her sunglasses off and held out her hand to each of them. Her eyes were puffy. She didn't look like she'd gotten much sleep either. Then again, she was used to sleeping in the daytime. "Thank you, Devon. That's so kind of you. Lulu and Hope, nice to meet you ladies. I appreciate your help."

Lulu just stood there, clutching her hands in front of her belly, frozen.

A flushed Hope managed a quiet, "No problem."

Devon seemed a bit nervous, too. It was subtle, but I noticed. He cleared his throat. "Elle and I both understand how a dog becomes part of your family. And I'm so sorry for the loss of your dog nanny."

Talia nodded. "Thank you. When she comes back home, Ginger's going to be just devastated that Diggs isn't here. He'd actually get down on the floor to play with her. Such a caring person. Please sit." She took the loveseat. Her gaze caught on Ginger's bed and fresh tears sprang to her swollen eyes. She closed them for a moment and took a deep breath. "I've been wracking my brain all night. Trying to think of who would take Ginger if it wasn't Sammy."

"Sammy's her ex," I explained to the room.

"We know," Hope and Lulu said in tandem.

Of course, I'm sure everyone on the planet knew, whether they wanted to or not. The scandal was inescapable.

Devon spoke up. "Sorry I have to ask, but you're absolutely sure Ginger didn't just run away? Maybe was frightened by the loud noise of glass breaking?"

Talia tilted her head slightly. "Well, I can't be one hundred percent sure. And believe me, I would prefer that scenario to thinking someone took her. I'd love to believe it, but she was in such a fragile state with her false pregnancy. She'd never abandon her green squeaky frog. In her mind, it was her puppy. She was such a good little mother."

I felt my face grow hot as I thought about how I'd flung it across the room, forcing Talia to fetch it.

"All right." Devon had his hands locked together, his elbows on his knees. "Elle said you told the detectives there was a custody battle with your ex-husband over the dogs and he lost. Do you believe he'd use force to take Ginger?"

"I honestly don't know," Talia said. "He definitely had a temper and, as you know, he was a professional fighter. If he tried to take Ginger from Diggs, Diggs would've defended her with his life. But no," she shook her head, "I can't believe Sammy's actually capable of murder."

"You'd be surprised what people are capable of." Devon's eyes blazed for a moment.

I wondered if he was thinking of his own parents' murders. They'd been killed because they found out a crooked jockey was doping their horses back in Dublin to win races. He'd hired two hitmen to smash into their boat and make it look like an accident. Senseless.

Devon rubbed his hands on his jeans. "Detective Vargas is floating the theory that Diggs's death may've been the result of the dognapping getting' out of hand. That Diggs wasn't actually the target. Do you have reason to believe your ex is on Moon Key?"

Talia gathered her hair over one shoulder and began to twist it nervously. "No, but I've not kept up with his whereabouts since our divorce eighteen months ago. We used to holiday here together though. He'd know I was here if he wanted to take Ginger."

I remembered the one odd thing about their divorce. Every detail had been splashed all over the Internet, except one. No one could pin down who he was having an affair with. I wondered if Talia ever found out? I couldn't imagine living my life with that kind of scrutiny, and couldn't blame her for living her life at night. It was probably the only time she had peace.

Devon glanced at me. "That's the first thing we'll check on then." Then his attention was back on Talia. "Anyone else?"

Talia's face pinked. She squirmed and leaned forward. As she was about to say something, Marcel entered and began to pass out the beverages from his tray.

"Thanks, Marcel." I watched as Talia leaned back into the sofa and took a sip from her coffee cup. She'd obviously changed her mind about whatever she was going to say. Was there someone else she was afraid to mention? We couldn't force it out of her. Hopefully she'd tell us soon if there was.

"You mentioned your neighbor, Nell?" I asked.

Talia turned to me. "Yeah. I can see her taking Ginger out of spite, but I really can't see her killing Diggs."

"Maybe we're looking at this from the wrong angle," Lulu said, a hand resting protectively on her belly. She did this a lot lately. I wondered if that meant she was going to be an overprotective mother. "What if it's not about Talia or Ginger at all? Did Diggs have any enemies? Anyone that would want to hurt him?"

Talia's eyes widened. "Diggs? Absolutely not. Diggs is... was one of those people who everyone took to immediately. That's why I'd hired him. I can't imagine anyone wanting to hurt him. He was just the gentlest soul on the planet. He loved my dogs like they were his own."

"How long had he been with you?" Hope asked, leaning forward.

"About eighteen months. I hired him right after my divorce. He was great company. He spent all his time with me and the dogs." She closed her eyes and struggled to compose herself. "He was just as devastated as I was when we lost Holly. He'll be missed."

I reached over and squeezed her hand. It was all I could think to do. She opened her eyes and the raw pain reflected there broke my heart. I suddenly felt the need for action. We had to do something.

I set my cup on the coffee table and rubbed my hands together. "I think it's time to get out there. We'll start our search around this area, then split up into teams. Devon and I will head east toward the Pampered Pup. Hope, you and Lulu can head west toward the Villas. We just keep going until we meet up on the other side of the island. I've got some of the ladies from doga class starting around nine this morning to scour the golf course in the middle. Talia, you're going to need to stay here in case Ginger finds her way back home. Any questions?"

Everyone stood, anxious to get going.

Talia trailed behind us as we made our way to the front door, her arms folded across her slim stomach. A single tear rolled down her cheek as she said goodbye. She wiped at it with the back of her hand. "Thank you, everyone."

Devon turned back. "One more question, Ms. Hill. Who created the statue of Holly for you?"

"It was Brentwood Glass Studio in Miami."

"Thank you."

I gave Talia's shoulder.a light squeeze. "We'll get her back home. I promise." As she nodded in agreement, I really hoped I could keep that promise.

FIVE

We searched every inch of Moon Key, knocking on doors and asking residents to check their properties, crawled along every perfectly manicured bush calling Ginger's name. We looked under every parked car, on every docked boat, in every parking garage, beneath every beach cabana and inside every business, where we also handed out flyers. We'd only stopped at lunchtime to feed our own dogs. By the time dusk began to fall, we were all exhausted, starving and feeling more than a little defeated.

We sat at the clubhouse and were slouched around a table, discouraged and waiting for our food.

"She couldn't have just disappeared. She's here somewhere," I moaned, rubbing my aching calf under the table.

"I hate to bring this up," Lulu said, "but if someone did actually grab her, they could've taken her off the island. She could be anywhere by now."

I didn't like the dark circles under Lulu's eyes. I should've sent her home hours ago to rest.

"Unfortunately you're right," Devon grunted. "Elle and I will go have a chat with the guard at the ferry terminal after we eat. You two have done all you can for tonight. You should head home."

"How many guards are there?" Lulu asked.

"One for the day shift and one for the night shift," Hope answered. "You'll have to talk to them both. In case the dognapper waited until morning to smuggle Ginger off of Moon Key. Though, they could've also used a private boat, but there's nothing to be done in that case."

My heart dropped as their words sank into my tired brain. I didn't want to believe Ginger had been taken, let alone taken off Moon Key. But our failure to find her today only solidified that as a possibility. Unless she'd decided to go for a swim, which I didn't want to think about either.

I barely tasted my *Gnocchi di zucca* pasta as we ate in silence. A growing dinner crowd surrounded us, people laughing, drinking and enjoying the holiday environment. I had a feeling none of us at the table would be able to join in the Christmas cheer if we didn't get Ginger back for Talia. Funny, we didn't even know her. She was just one of those people who seemed so fragile and full of goodness that you wanted to protect her from pain. Plus, I couldn't even imagine Buddha being lost, especially at Christmastime. My resolve stiffened inside me like hardening glue. We had to get Ginger back. There was no other option.

We sent Hope home and said our goodbyes to Lulu at the ferry terminal. "I'll come back in the morning. We'll try again."

I hugged Lulu and put on my best stern face. "You just get some rest. I'll give you a call and let you know what we're doing."

We waited our turn and then approached the guard house. Frank's wide smile greeted us. "Hey Mr. Devon. Boarding this evening?"

"Actually, no, we just have a quick question for ya." Devon handed the flyer to Frank through the guardhouse window. "Talia Hill's dog has gone missing. She's a white terrier and we were wondering if you saw anyone board the ferry with her last night?"

"Talia Hill huh?" he whistled, his eyes taking on a dreamy look.

Devon tapped on the flyer to redirect his attention. "Her dog… did you see anyone take it off the island?" He wasn't usually short with people, but he seemed to be growing more worried by the hour.

Frank scrutinized the photo of Ginger and then shrugged. "I didn't see a white dog like that, no. But then again, I don't really check what's inside folk's carriers, and there were more than a few carriers."

Devon nodded slowly and glanced up at the corner of the guardhouse. "You've got security tapes. How long do you keep 'em?"

Frank leaned his forearms on the counter. "They get sent off every twenty-four hours to a digital storage facility and we record over them. He held up an aged hand. " But I know what you're going to ask and no can do. This island is very protective of its privacy. I've been down this road before. The police would have to request the tapes."

Devon glanced at me and nodded. "No problem." He started to leave and then turned back. "You know Miss Hill's ex, Sammy Salazar, yeah?"

"Of course. Best UFC fighter ever."

"He come through here in the last few days?"

Frank grinned. "Now, Mr. Devon, you know I can't tell you that either."

Devon smiled back but I could see the frustration tightening the corners of his eyes. "The police need to do the asking. Right. Goodnight, Frank."

By the time we pulled the Jeep into the driveway, the timer had lit up the Christmas lights and decorations. All the holiday cheer was depressing.

I turned to Devon. "Do you mind letting the dogs out? I'm just going to run over to Talia's and let her know we didn't find Ginger. That's not news I want to give her over the phone."

He hesitated. "Sure."

I took in his wrinkled brow and tightened jaw. "What's wrong?"

Before opening the door he shot me a meaningful look. "Just be careful. I'm still not sure what's going on here."

I gave him a quick kiss and pulled the mace out of my bag. "I'm armed, don't worry."

He'd bought me a gun before we even started officially dating, but I'd never grown confident I could actually pull the trigger, and I'd learned the hard way hesitation could get me killed. Besides, I wasn't worried. My childhood dog, Angel, always showed up in spirit form to warn me when I was about to be in danger, and there was no sign of her... yet.

He wrapped one arm around my waist, pulling me closer for a lingering kiss and then sighed. "I will always worry. You seem to excel at finding trouble."

Talia's door swung open before I even reached her front porch. She raced toward me. "Elle! Did you find Ginger?"

I watched her eyes flick from me to my empty Beetle and then fall in devastation. My heart fell with her. "I'm so sorry."

She steeled herself. "I know. Thank you for trying. Can you come in for a minute? It's just so... quiet without Ginger and Diggs here."

"Sure."

We sat there drinking Marcel's hot chocolate and swapping stories about our dogs, our childhoods, our relationships. I found myself forgetting that she was a big movie star. When I finally glanced at my phone, I was startled to see how late it was. "Oh, I'm sorry, I've stayed so late. I should go."

She stretched. "No worries, Elle. This is my daytime, remember?"

I smiled. "Yes, but I'll be useless in class tomorrow. Plus I'll need the energy to continue our search. We aren't giving up looking for Ginger."

"Well, I do appreciate you taking my mind off of her for a while. I don't feel so hopeless now."

She walked me to the door. When I opened it to leave, I squealed and jumped back.

A large man in a ball cap and black t-shirt stood there glaring at us.

Instinctively, I reached in my purse and grabbed my mace. My shaking hand managed to aim it at his face, but before I could push the trigger, he reached out like lightning and snatched it from me.

An amused grin spread on his lips, right under a large scar on his cheek.

I felt Talia's hand on my arm. "It's all right, Elle. It's just Sammy." Now her expression grew dark and her fists were perched on her hips. "What in heaven's name are you doing at my door at one in the morning?"

He handed me back my mace with a smirk. "What? Like you wouldn't be up? I know your schedule, remember? Anyway, I heard about what happened with Diggs. It's all over the news. And how Ginger's gone missing. I'm really sorry. Thought I'd come to Moon Key tonight to see if I could help."

Talia crossed her arms and seemed to be in control, but I could feel her shaking next to me. This guy really got to her. "Bring your girlfriend with you?"

His gray eyes registered hurt within a sharp-planed face. "Can we just work together on this without any snide comments? Ginger means a lot to me, too. You know that."

Talia lifted her chin. "How do I know you didn't take her and this is all for show?"

Sammy grunted and then must've realized she was serious. He glared at her. "I didn't take her, Talia."

They stared at each other for an uncomfortably long time. I suddenly felt like a third wheel and took a few steps back out of the way.

Finally, Talia sighed. "Fine. Come in." She turned and hugged me. "Go on, Elle, I'll be all right."

I wasn't sure about the wisdom of leaving Talia with her very large, very-good-at-violence ex-husband. But I wasn't sure I had a choice either. I'd just be sure to check on her in the morning.

What a mess.

SIX

"Good morning, everyone." I sat on the wood floor of my studio at the Pampered Pup in lotus pose, my hands running over Buddha's belly and waiting for the morning doga class to get settled on their mats.

The dogs seemed extra wound up this morning, playing and running around the studio. A sharp bark echoed off the walls, and another joined in. Feeding off their owners' holiday energy, no doubt.

"Morning, Elle." Beth Anne Wilkins settled in on her mat in the front. Her white and gray Shitzu, Shakespeare, was trying to climb her chest to lick her face and nip at the end of her thick, brown ponytail. She and Shakespeare were wearing matching long-sleeve red Lycra shirts. "Down," she admonished. Then rolling her eyes at me she added, "I left him at home all day yesterday while we were searching the golf course, so he's being extra clingy this morning." She managed to get him to sit in front of her. "So, any news on Talia Hill's dog?"

The other ladies quieted down and turned their attention to me.

I shook my head. "Not yet, but she really appreciates everyone who came out yesterday to help search."

"What do the police think?" Violet fluffed up her spiky, red hair with one hand, while the other rested on her neurotic Weimaraner, Ghost. His haunches were planted firmly in her small lap. "Do they think someone dognapped her?"

I leaned forward, rubbing Buddha's warm ears between my fingers. "I don't know. But I don't think finding Ginger is a priority for them. They're more concerned with finding the dog nanny's killer."

"Seems like if they find Ginger, they find the killer. Do you need our help again today?" Whitley asked. Her gray eyes shone with concern behind wire-framed glasses. She stroked her greyhound, Maddox's, side. She'd dressed Maddox in a red t-shirt with a Christmas tree embroidered on the back. Whitley was in black, though, her standard dress. "I can't imagine not knowing where Maddox was, if he was even alive. So awful."

"It is," I agreed. She was the rational one of the group, so if she was concerned about Ginger still being alive, we all should be. I glanced down at Buddha. "I'm just not sure there's anything we can do besides canvas the island again. Devon's going to talk to Detective Vargas today about getting a look at the security tapes at the ferry terminal. If someone did take Ginger off of Moon Key, maybe the tapes will show that."

Beth Anne was leaning back on her hands, her long legs were outstretched and crossed at the ankles. Shakespeare had wandered off. She was frowning. "Let's hope not. She could be anywhere by now."

She was a big fan of mystery novels, so her mind went to worst-case scenario. My therapist called it catastrophic thinking. Still, she had a point.

We were all quiet for a moment as the last of the women straggled in, rolled out their mats and got settled with their dogs. I sent up a little prayer to the universe that Ginger was still safe and sound on Moon Key. Then it was time to get our doggie-zen on.

"All right, everyone, let's start with some cat and dog tilts. Knees and hands equal distance apart on the mat."

I had a hard time keeping my mind from wandering back to Talia's predicament during class. She hadn't answered her phone when I'd called to check on her this morning. I tried to convince myself that was because morning was her bedtime. Maybe she was getting some much needed sleep. But, I couldn't push away the image of Sammy showing up and scaring the bezeezuz out of me last night.

Devon had been worried, too, when I'd come home and told him about Sammy just showing up at her door. But he'd said she knew him better than we did, so if she wasn't worried, we shouldn't be either. Tell that to my over-active imagination.

I checked my phone as soon as class was over. Sure enough there was a text from Devon. Salma was already planning to get the security tapes from the ferry terminal today to look for any suspicious behavior. I took a deep breath. Okay, that's something. Movement. Things are happening.

"Hey, Elle... are y'all going to the board meeting tonight?" Beth Anne asked as she scooped up

Shakespeare. He licked her chin with his postage-stamp sized tongue.

"Wasn't planning on it, why?" I'd rather be anywhere else, and I didn't consider myself a Moon Key resident anyway, so I never paid attention to board meetings.

She stroked Shakespear's head, her champagne colored eyes sparkling with good humor. "Should be an entertaining one is all. There's a big hullabaloo over the budget spending on the Christmas decorations. The cost has doubled this year and a few of the board members are accusing Eva Gold of changing November's minutes to say they approved of the price increase, which she probably did. Might get your mind off of finding Ginger for a while. Sometimes it helps to get away from a problem, so you can see it fresh afterwards."

Violet had walked up and nodded in agreement. "Trust me. You don't want to miss this one. Bring popcorn."

—◦◦◦◦—

Devon and I sat beside Beth Anne, who'd saved us two seats up front at the board meeting. Violet and Whitley sat to her left. They'd actually brought popcorn. We'd decided to come after all, in hopes of being able to speak to the community about Ginger.

I glanced around. The room was packed and people did not look happy. Someone was wearing heavy cologne that was making me feel both nauseous and claustrophobic. I started to feel lightheaded, my heart skipping beats. Maybe this was a mistake. I didn't do well in crowds.

"I'm just going to run to the restroom real quick," I said to Devon, before jumping up and escaping.

I shut myself in an end stall and forced myself to take deep, slow breaths. Digging in my bag, I found a hairband and pulled my mass of auburn hair up into a messy bun to get it off my sweaty neck. Just as I was feeling calmer, I heard the door creak open.

A women's voice said, "Well, at least that tacky dog statue is gone now."

"What do you want, Eva? I already agreed to do what you asked."

Tacky dog statue? They were talking about Talia! I pulled my feet up out of view.

"I know. I just wanted to be sure you remembered your promise before the meeting started. Think of this as a friendly reminder."

"A friendly reminder? It's blackmail, Eva, and you know it," the second woman's voice rose in volume.

Who is the second woman? I tried to peek through the crack in the door, but I couldn't see them. They were standing out of my view.

Eva chuckled. "Call it whatever you want, dear. See you in there."

The door squeaked back opened. After a growl of frustration from the second woman and a second door squeak, I was alone again.

What in heavens was all that about?

I waited a full minute before coming out of the stall. As I walked back into the meeting room, I glanced at the board members now seated at the table in front.

"Which one is Eva Gold?" I asked Beth Anne, as I sat back down.

She flicked her long hair over one shoulder and leaned closer to me. "The heavy-set Russian lady in the middle with the dark pixie cut. The one looking down on us like we're her subjects."

I narrowed my eyes. "She does look intimidating."

"She's not all bark either. She once rammed her golfcart into the side of Brock Sieger's brand new Lexus. No one was sure what that argument was about, but she's also destroyed more than one person's new landscaping with that cart, because it wasn't approved through the HOA first. She wields it like a weapon."

"Not someone you want to get on the wrong side of then," I noted. "So, tell me about the rest of the board."

I caught a whiff of Beth Anne's fruity shampoo as she happily leaned in closer. "The old, grumpy guy on Eva's left is Sterling Bale. He disagrees with everyone on the board about everything, much to Eva's irritation. She can't control him. It's mostly Sterling and Nell Barnwell, the stocky gray-haired lady on the end over there, who oppose Eva on everything."

"Nell Barnwell," I whispered. "That's Talia's neighbor. The one she said hated her dogs." I eyed the woman. Despite the gray hair, she didn't look fragile at all. She definitely looked like she could give Diggs a good fight.

"Yep. Nell's just a bit off her rocker so no one controls her. She believes she hales from British royalty and says whatever's on her mind. I like her, personally. The two members who *sometimes* butt heads with Eva are Jata—who just seems out for a fight once in a while—and Sunny Spillman, the petite blonde at the other end. Sunny doesn't seem to like conflict though, so she picks her battles and manages to win some of them, even with her soft-spoken ways." She smiled as she stared at the small woman with admiration. "It's actually fun to watch. She has a way of manipulating Eva when she wants to. Talks her into thinking things are her idea. Pretty impressive. Anyway, the other two— Priya and Jackson—are Eva's yes man and woman. They're good friends and Eva has side meetings at her house with them, to make sure they're all on the same page before the meetings. Questions?"

I shook my head absent-mindedly, trying to figure out which woman Eva had talked to in the restroom and was blackmailing. Maybe I would recognize her voice.

"Here we go," Beth Anne chuckled as Eva Gold raised her hand to quiet the room.

I smirked at her. She was enjoying the possibility of drama a little too much.

"Let the record reflect tonight's meeting is beginning at six p.m," Eva said.

The willowy, dark-skinned woman to her right, wearing bright orange lipstick—Jata was it?—handed her a folder of papers.

Eva held it in front of her. "We'll start with approval of last month's meeting minutes. All in favor of approval raise your hand."

Everyone on the board, except Sterling Bale, raised their hand. He pushed his palms into the table to help himself sit taller, but he was still looking up at Eva. His head wobbled with the effort. "Maybe we should read 'em, make sure they weren't altered."

"Now, Sterling." Eva's voice took on the air of an adult being patient with a child. "That conflict is on our agenda to discuss at the end of the meeting, which we won't get to for hours if we have to read November's minutes aloud."

He waved a knotty, veined hand dismissively at her. "Fine."

A tight smile pulled Eva's mouth in a thin line. "All right. Minutes approved. Let's move on. First some old business. Last month the community brought a petition to the board to increase the number of tropical fish allowed from fifteen to twenty-five. You all will be pleased to know that the board has approved that request, and the bylaws will be changed to reflect the new amount of allowed fish."

There was a smattering of applause. Devon and I shared an amused grin. Seriously, do they come into your house and count your fish? Just the logistics of trying to count a bunch of moving targets struck me as ridiculous.

My mind drifted in and out during the next hour as they talked about things like landscaping and repairing the guest dock. I'd narrowed the blackmailee down to either Nell Barnwell or Sunny Spillman. Jata and Priya both had distinguishable accents. Devon squeezed my knee when I got fidgety. Maybe coming here wasn't the best idea. We should be out canvasing the island for Ginger. But then, the discussion about November's controversial minutes erupted.

"You know darn well we never approved Gold Holiday Lights's exorbitant raise in fees to decorate this year, Eva," Nell Barnwell said. "They've almost doubled."

Someone in the audience shouted behind us. "We should be getting estimates from other companies."

"Yeah... ridiculous!" The audience rumbled, throwing out words like, "Need other estimates... favoritism... your brother."

Eva held up a hand, her dark eyes glittering with barely disguised anger. "Okay, everyone." She waited for them to calm down, her forearms resting on the table in front of her. "Can I speak?" Eventually everyone quieted down, but the tension was still thick as molasses in the room. "Listen, I realize you all think because it's my brother, Georgy, who owns Gold Holiday Lights that I'm giving them the contract no questions asked on their prices. But, I assure you, I have looked into other companies and, for what they are giving us, their price is more than fair."

She stood and walked over to the framed articles hanging on the wall beside the doorway. Sweeping her hand over the ones on the left, she said, "Besides, look what they do for us. These are ten years worth of Tampa Bay Times and Clearwater Gazette articles praising Moon Key for our contribution to the Christmas boat parade every year. Gushing about how much we add to the Christmas spirit of the community, how people drive for hours to bring their kids to the boat parade and witness Moon Key's spectacular Christmas show. I, for one, can't put a price on that kind of joy... can you?"

I glanced around. Some people still had their arms folded, unconvinced. But others had dropped their eyes and softened their shoulders.

Eva took her seat again. "Now, Sterling, I know you think you remember the vote going the other way..."

Beth Anne leaned in and whispered, "It did. Someone definitely changed the meeting minutes."

"So," Eva continued, "what I propose is we take another vote right now in front of the community so there's no confusion. All in favor of a public vote?" She glanced at the board.

Everyone raised their hand.

"Good. All in favor of Gold Lights keeping the contract to decorate Moon Key for Christmas?"

Priya and Jackson raised their hands in solidarity with Eva immediately. No surprise. That was three. They just needed one more for the majority. I scanned the table. Who would it be? Sterling had sat back in his chair and crossed his arms. Definitely not him. Jata and Nell didn't budge either. But then... Sunny Spillman sighed and raised her hand.

A small smile of victory twitched on Eva's lips. "Let the record show the majority has voted to renew Gold Holiday Lights's contract."

Sterling leaned forward and glared at Sunny. "Leave it up to a woman to change her mind."

So, it was her, Sunny Spillman, who Eva was blackmailing.

What does Eva have on her?

Sunny ignored Sterling. In fact her attention was on someone in the audience.

I followed her gaze to a handsome younger guy, probably in his late twenties. *Her son?* Had to be, though he didn't look much like her. He had thick, wavy black hair and a much larger frame. He offered her a sympathetic smile.

Eva cleared her throat loudly. "All right, now that that's settled, is there any business from the audience?"

"There is." Devon stood up and held up the flyer. "In case you haven't heard, Talia Hill's dog nanny was killed last night and her dog's gone missing. This is Ginger. She's a West Highland white terrier, about twenty pounds and was wearing a pink collar at the time of her disappearance. We'd like everyone to keep an eye out for her. If you have any information or spot the dog, please contact Clearwater police immediately. Thanks."

There was some murmuring that began to escalate in volume and energy. I glanced around to see if anyone was acting nervous or suspicious, but no one was that I could see.

Eva got the audience back under control to officially end the meeting. We waited as people began to gather by the door, some pairing up into smaller knots for private discussions.

Beth Anne shrugged. "I thought there'd be more arguing. Oh well."

"You seem disappointed," I teased her. "Don't worry, it was still worth it. I learned some interesting things. Like, they can limit the number of fish you own."

She rolled her eyes, reaching up to rub the tiny diamond snowflake necklace nestled at her throat. "Yeah, all pets are limited. You can have three domestic pets like cats or dogs or a combination of the two, two birds and one exotic pet like a lizard, hedgehog or a snake. God only knows why someone would want a snake as a pet, though."

Violet leaned over. "That reminds me. Before Nell Barnwell was voted on the board last year, she had a big fight with them about her two peacocks, because the board decided they should be classified as exotic pets instead of birds, allowing her only one. Eventually one of the birds disappeared which, as we know, she blamed on Talia dogs."

Beth Anne nodded. "The feathers were scattered all over Talia's front yard. Talia insisted someone set her dogs up. If that's true, I'd bet on Eva. She's the kind of person that gets what she wants at all costs. I wouldn't put it past her to get rid of Nell's peacock herself."

"Really?" I scanned the room, finding Nell easily. She was a tall, strong-looking woman that towered above the group of people she was in conversation with. "Talia did mention that Nell hated her dogs. You think Eva set them up, huh?"

Violet tucked the empty popcorn bag into her Louis Vuitton purse. "I just wouldn't be shocked, that's all."

We stood up. The room had cleared enough to leave without feeling like we were part of a herd of sheep. That's when I noticed Sunny and the young, dark-haired man standing by the window chatting. He sure was a snazzy dresser in his black dress slacks and mint green button-down shirt.

She had her forehead resting on his chest, her shoulders slumped, her fists clutching the opening of his taylored blazer. She looked upset. Probably about Eva blackmailing her into changing her vote.

He leaned down and whispered something in her ear. Then he raised her chin with an index finger and kissed her. Full on the mouth.

Definitely not her son.

Violet saw my mouth drop and followed my gaze. Then she chuckled. "I really need to get the name of that dating site Sunny uses. The older she gets, the younger her male companions get."

I shook off the images that Violet's comment sent racing through my mind. "Hey, guys, come here." I waved Violet, Beth Anne and Whitley into a tighter circle. "So, I overheard a conversation between Eva and Sunny in the restroom. At least, I'm pretty sure it was Sunny. Eva was blackmailing Sunny, which I believe is why she changed her vote so Eva's brother could keep the decorating contract. Do any of you know what that could've been about?"

The three women glanced at each other.

Beth Anne was the one that spoke up. "Nope, but it'll sure be fun to try and find out."

SEVEN

I left the house early Tuesday morning so I could stop by and check on Talia before my morning doga class. I was really uncomfortable with the fact I'd left her with her ex. When I pulled up, I was surprised to see a security golf cart parked in her driveway.

Did something else happen? Did Sammy hurt her? Is that why she didn't answer her phone yesterday?

By the time I got Buddha to jump down from the passenger's seat and rushed to the front door, my pulse was racing like a jackrabbit and I was furious with myself. The door opened, and I stammered at Marcel. "Is she okay? I'm so sorry. I shouldn't have just left like that."

He stared at me for a moment in confusion and then opened the door further to let me in. "She's in the great room. I'm sure she'd like to see you."

I hurried Buddha through the house to find Talia in tears on the sofa and Alex Harwick seated stiffly in the chair, looking very uncomfortable. He lifted a hand in greeting.

Ignoring him, I rushed over to sit beside Talia, releasing Buddha's leash. "Talia? What happened?"

Her eyes were wide with shock and her face was drained of color. She opened her mouth to speak but a sudden sob choked her. She held out her hand instead.

"Oh no," I whispered. There, clutched in her hand, was Ginger's pink collar. "What... what does this mean? Is she..." I couldn't even finish the thought. "Where did you get it?"

Buddha snuck his nose in the collar's direction, sniffing hard. He tilted his head toward me, his brown eyes full of questions. I rested a hand on his back to comfort us both.

Still sniffling, Talia pointed to a white sheet of paper lying on top of a yellow envelope. "Someone put it in my mailbox."

I went to reach for it but Alex stopped me. "Don't touch it, Elle. It might have fingerprints or something on it. We're waiting for the Clearwater police."

I nodded and slid down in front of the table, so I could read it without touching it. It was a plain white piece of typing paper with a computer printed message:

I have Ginger. A boat with a yellow flag will be waiting at the guest dock at midnight on Friday. Hand over one million dollars in unmarked bills to the driver. He will know nothing and receive instructions only after he is safely on his way without police interference. If he is followed, I will know and she will die. If he doesn't make it to his drop off spot, she will die. Once I have the money, I will return her safely. You have my word.

I slowly pushed myself back up onto the sofa, running through what this meant in my mind. Buddha rested his bulk against my shin with a huff, probably sensing the tension and anxiety in the room.

So, someone did dognap Ginger. For a million dollars? Is it the same person who killed Diggs? Or did Ginger run away and someone found her and decided to use the opportunity to extort Talia?

"Do you think this person is feeding her?" Talia choked out on a sob. "She must be so worried about her puppies."

I grabbed her hands. They were ice cold and still had a death-grip on the collar. Was she in shock? "Let's concentrate on the fact that she's alive. The good thing about dogs is they live in the moment, right? So, once this is all over, and she's back home safe and sound, she won't even remember it. She'll bounce back and be her happy self in no time." I paused, and then asked softly. "I assume you want to pay the ransom?"

Her eyes widened. "Of course. I would give him every bit of money I have to get her back."

I nodded. "And whoever took her knows that." I thought about the two suspects we had so far, Sammy and Nell. They were already weathly, so it wouldn't make sense for either of them to ask for ransom money. Unless it was a ploy to throw the police off their trail.

The doorbell chimed. Alex stood up as Detective Vargas and a uniformed officer strolled into the great room, looking none too happy. She took in me and Talia on the sofa and then glanced down at the ransom note. "This it?"

Talia nodded.

Salma turned to the officer. "Bag it. The envelope and collar, too."

Talia clutched the collar to her chest.

Salma softened her voice. "Ms. Hill, we may be able to pull prints or DNA off that and get her home faster."

Talia reluctantly handed the officer Ginger's collar, which he deposited in a separate bag while sneaking a few glances at her, his fair skin reddening. I'd all but forgotten she was a movie star, until I saw other people's reactions to her like that.

"Get a cheek swab from Miss Hill so we can separate her DNA from any we find on the collar." Then Salma turned to Alex. "Thanks, Mr. Harwick. We'll take it from here."

Alex seemed more than happy to duck out, but as he passed he said, "Elle, can I talk to you for a sec."

I cringed inwardly. Having a conversation with Alex Harwick was the last thing on earth I wanted to do. "Sure."

Glancing back, as I followed Alex out, I saw the officer hand Salma the letter safely encased in plastic.

I folded my arms as I stood in front of him, keeping my distance. "What's up?"

He took a card out of his pocket, looking sheepish, which was very unlike him. Usually over-confidence oozed from him like a poisonous gas. "You don't have to answer right now. But, I have two tickets to the HOA Christmas party next week and would like you to come with me." He handed me the card. "Just give me a call and let me know."

I took it reluctantly, shoving it into my jacket pocket. There was no way I wanted to spend an evening with Alex Harwick, but I remembered my plan to get close to him, since he could help in putting Devon's parents' murderers behind bars. Alex had overheard one of the hitmen bragging at a bar right before Devon's parents were killed, but he'd recanted his testimony.

Besides, the HOA? If I could learn what information Eva Gold had used to blackmail Sunny with, or talk to Nell Barnwell, that would be a bonus. Still, I couldn't bring myself to say yes. "I'll let you know."

I quickly made my way back to Talia's side.

Salma was just handing the ransom note back to the officer with a neutral expression. "Ms. Hill, I know you've probably already decided to pay the ransom demand, but I feel it's my duty to inform you that paying the ransom doesn't mean you'll get Ginger back. In fact, in most kidnappings the victim is not recovered alive. And that's a human. For an animal..." she let the unfinished thought hang in the air.

I glanced at Talia. Her eyes widened in horror but then determination replaced that. "I have to take the chance, no matter how small, that he'll release her unharmed."

Salma pursed her lips and shifted on her feet. "I also have to inform you that, while I can justify a print and DNA request on these items, the State Attorney's office most likely won't authorize the use of much larger resources to help with the exchange of money for Ginger. Unless, perhaps we can convince them that the ransom demand is definitely coming from Diggs's assailant, but even then..." She shook her head.

"But, the dognapper killed Diggs to get Ginger... isn't that obvious?" Talia asked.

"Unfortunately, no." Salma hesitated and then continued to explain. "Ginger could've been scared off by the altercation between Diggs and his assailant. Someone could've found her and decided to make you pay to get her back. A crime of opportunity. Seems like it'd be someone who knows you and your passion for your dogs. Otherwise, I think they would've asked for a much more reasonable ransom amount for an animal."

I watched Talia grow defensive at Salma's use of the word "animal" or "reasonable" and then deflate. Salma walked over and took a seat in the chair that Alex had vacated. "Ms. Hill, you mentioned before that you and your ex-husband had a custody battle over the dogs, correct?" Talia nodded. "What about over money? Did he want more money than he received in the divorce settlement?"

Talia shook her head. "No, he has his own money. There were no issues around that. Why?"

"Well, we've gone over the security tapes from the ferry, and it seems he arrived on Moon Key Saturday... the same evening Mr. Diggs was killed." She paused and let that sink in.

Talia looked confused. "But, that's not possible. He showed up at my door Sunday evening. Said he'd just arrived... he lied?" An angry burst of energy colored her cheeks.

"That's true. I was here and I heard him say he'd just arrived," I agreed.

"Well, we weren't able to figure out where he's staying on the island. No one has a record of him checking in, and there's no sign of him leaving on the security tapes. Is there an alias he uses that you know of?"

Anger had stiffened her spine. "Yes, Chuck Lee."

Salma wrote that down in her notebook. "Okay, we'll check the hotels again with that name. Meanwhile, you call me if he shows up here. He's the number one suspect in my book. He's obviously strong enough to kill Diggs with one blow to the head and shatter the statue. Plus he has motive to take Ginger. And now that we know he lied about when he arrived on Moon Key, well that just adds to my suspicion."

Talia pulled out her cell phone. "Hang on. Let me try to call him." She dialed and we all waited. After a few rings she shook her head in disappointment then left a message. "Sammy, call me as soon as you get this." She looked like she wanted to say more, but she gritted her teeth and hung up.

I thought about the ransom note. "But Salma, the ransom note says he'll know if the boat is being followed. Wouldn't that require an accomplice?"

"If he's telling the truth, yes. Most likely it's an empty threat, though. Most likely the person who shows up for the ransom will be the one who has Ginger. Why would he risk getting anyone else involved? He'd have to split the money."

I bit the inside of my lip. "True. But if it was Sammy who took Ginger, and he does have an accomplice, maybe that's who he's staying with on Moon Key."

"I can't take that chance with Ginger's life," Talia said. "I'll follow his instructions. I'll give him the money and no one will follow the boat, as he requested. If you arrest him, he may never tell us where Ginger is."

Salma looked like she was about to disagree but changed her mind. "That's your prerogative. We'll let you know if we find your ex on the island. Meanwhile, you let us know if he contacts you again and stay alert." She rose to go.

I checked the time on my phone. Yikes. "I'm sorry, Talia." I picked up Buddha's leash. "I have to get going to class." She sat motionless, staring at Ginger's empty bed, the despair palpable in her frozen expression. "Talia?"

Her eyes slowly met mine. My heart ached at the pain I saw there. "Hey, let me talk to Devon. Maybe we can help the police find Sammy faster. Devon's a really good P.I." She nodded stiffly and I reached down and gave her a gentle hug. "Hang in there."

On the short hop around the island to the Pampered Pup Resort I called Devon and filled him in on the ransom note and the fact that Sammy had actually arrived on Moon Key the night Diggs had been killed. "Talia said he sometimes uses an alias at hotels... Chuck Lee. Do you think you can find him?"

"I can try but it doesn't really make sense. He knows her schedule, knew that she'd be up at that time of night. Why wouldn't he have waited until she was asleep to take Ginger? If that was his motive, to get the dog back."

"Guess we'll have to ask him. But, we have to find him first."

EIGHT

After my second doga class of the day, I'd brought out the box of dog toys and dumped them out in the middle of the studio. The dogs were currently running wild, playing and chasing each other while their owners lounged around and chatted. They deserved it today. The ladies had done a great job getting the dogs to relax during class. Now they got to burn off some holiday energy.

I crossed the studio floor, stepping around mats, and being careful not to step on my smaller four-legged clients, to check my phone. I was supposed to be meeting Devon for lunch at Café Belle—which was named after one of Priscilla Moon's late Yorkies.

Priscilla was the billionaire heiress and dog lover extraordinaire, who'd spared no expense redecorating and revamping Moon Key when she'd bought the island nearly fifty years ago. The story was, while vacationing with her three Yorkshire terriers, she'd been told she couldn't bring them into establishments. So, she simply bought the island and fired everyone, creating a dog-friendly slice of paradise and turning the island's once posh human-only hotel into the Pampered Pup Spa & Resort.

There was a missed call from a number I didn't recognize and a new message.

A no-nonsense female voice said, "Hi, this is Marcy Jenkins from Clearwater General. I'm looking for a Ms. Elvis Pressley. Can you please return my call at this number."

I cringed and squeezed my eyes shut. This had to have something to do with my mother. She was the only one who called me by my given name, Elvis. My hand was shaking as I dialed the number and asked for Marcy Jenkins.

"Ms. Pressley?" she asked when she came on the line.

"This is she," I said.

"You're the person listed on Ms. Vera Pressley's emergency contact."

"Yes, I'm her daughter." My heart jumped and I glanced down at Buddha, who had followed me over and was leaning against my leg. "Is something wrong?"

"I'm afraid your mother has suffered a heart attack. She's here at Clearwater General in surgery now. It's limited-access coronary artery surgery, which usually has an excellent outcome."

"Oh God! I'll be there as soon as I can."

Devon sat with me in the waiting room, both of us sipping cold, bitter coffee out of Styrofoam cups. My guilt was just as bitter. I should've tried harder to get her to take care of herself, to get her to stop living on alcohol and sugar. Her arteries were probably full of Twinkie filling.

"Hey, I know that look, Elle." Devon shifted in the plastic chair and ducked his head to catch my eye. "I'll not let you blame yourself for this. Your ma is a grown woman and made her own health choices."

I blinked, surprised, for one, that he knew me so well and two that my guilt actually responded to him and eased its grip on me a little. I slipped my hand into his. "Thanks, I needed to hear that."

His phone buzzed. He lifted my hand to his mouth and pressed a kiss to the back of it before answering, "Devon Burke." After listening for a minute he said, "thanks," and then disconnected. "That was Salma. They have a definite cause of death for Diggs. Seems the killer used a claw hammer to deliver a blow to the temple, rupturing the temporal artery and causing sudden death. From the angle of the blow, Diggs appears to have been facing his assailant, so the killer, who would've been about six-foot, was holding the hammer in his or her left hand when they struck the blow."

I grimaced at the thought. "So, we have two clues. The killer is left-handed and about six-foot tall." I leaned into Devon's shoulder for comfort. Then raising my head I added, "I guess if there's any silver lining in all this, it's that Diggs didn't suffer."

Devon readjusted his position in the chair, angling his body more towards me. "The motive here had to be Ginger, grabbing her for the ransom money. What other possible motive could there be? Unless Diggs was involved in something shady, and his death had nothin' to do with Ginger." He shook his head. He seemed to be arguing with himself. "Can't be, though. Salma said they've been looking into his past and doing phone interviews. He's clean as a whistle and everyone says the same thing about him, all around nice fella. No recent relationships, his life revolved around his clients' dogs. He truly loved his job. Bloody Boy Scout, he was."

I lifted his hand, examining his tan fingers, clean, square nailbeds, then entwined our fingers. "Well, we only have three more days to find out for Ginger's sake. Salma warned Talia that even if she pays the ransom, the odds of her getting Ginger back alive are slim to none."

"Ms. Pressley?" A tired-looking doctor in green scrubs walked toward us with a smile, his mask pulled down below his chin, his gray hair sticking up awkwardly above his temple. "Your mother is out of surgery. Everything went well."

We both stood up. "Can I see her?" I asked.

"She"ll be in ICU overnight. She'll still be pretty out of it, so I suggest you wait until tomorrow to visit her, when she's moved to a regular room. Tonight the best thing you can do for her would be to go home and get some rest yourself."

I nodded, relieved the surgery went well but feeling anxious about what came next. "How long will she be in the hospital?"

He folded his hands in front of him and pursed his lips. "Three or four days. Then it would probably be best for someone to stay with her for a few days at home as she recovers."

Stay with her? I moaned to myself. There was no way I was going back to that house. I began to feel hives coming on. I scratched at my neck. "Thank you, Dr. Greene."

I leaned on Devon heavily on the way to the parking garage, enjoying the solidness of his form propping up my tired bones. I suddenly felt exhausted and fragile, thankful to have him to lean on and at the same time terrified one day I wouldn't. People leave each other all the time, especially people filled with wanderlust like Devon. I shouldn't get used to counting on him. Still, at the moment, I couldn't get up the energy to pull myself away from him.

"I can't go and stay with her when she comes home. I just can't." I trembled at the thought of being back in that house. Back in her world where I felt like an insecure kid again, my only job taking care of her needs. I'd never been able to find myself under her shadow. I was just starting to discover my own place in life, figure out where I belonged. The irony of finding that sense of belonging on Moon Key, the one place I definitely didn't belong, didn't escape me.

Devon pulled me tighter against him. "Well, then, she can just stay at the beach bungalow with us for a few days. We'll get a live-in nurse so you don't have to worry about anything."

I glanced up at him, at the sureness and kindness in his expression. "You wouldn't mind?"

He laughed softly, his blue eyes twinkling with good humor. "I think I can manage having her around for a few days."

As we arrived at the Jeep, I had to smile at his naivete. "You're tough but I'm not sure you're that tough, Mr. Burke."

—⁂—

Wednesday afternoon, between my second and third doga class at the Pampered Pup, I ran to the hospital to visit Mom. She was in a regular room but was sound asleep. I decided not to wake her. I didn't think I could hide the sadness I felt seeing her lying so helpless in those stiff, white sheets. Her skin was sallow and wrinkled, her slack lips revealing a rotten tooth. I hadn't noticed how old she'd grown. She looked twenty years older than she should.

Oh, Mom. What have you done to yourself?

I could do nothing. Wiping away the hot tears, I promised myself I'd visit again tomorrow. Right now I had another pressing problem. Only two more days until we knew Ginger's fate.

—❦—

My phone buzzed as I walked down the hall to the Pampered Pup acupuncture room to check on Buddha. He'd been favoring his back left leg the last few weeks. The vet couldn't find anything wrong with it and suggested it could just be a sprain or sore from our new, more strenuous exercise routine. So we'd backed off that, and I'd added a few acupuncture and massage sessions to his weekly routine. They seemed to be helping.

I stopped in the middle of the hallway when I saw the number. "Hey, Talia. Everything okay?"

"Yes, yes, as well as it can be. I was just wondering... I'm going crazy here with my own thoughts. Do you want to bring your friends over for a late dinner tonight? I'd like to thank them for their help and it would keep me from going insane." She chuckled but I could hear the strain of truth in her voice.

"Sure," I said without thinking. "What time?"

"Nine o'clock?"

"We'll be there."

Devon had somewhere else to be, but at nine o'clock Lulu, Hope, Beth Anne and I stood on Talia's front porch. Lulu held her homemade pecan pie, Beth Anne had a wine gift bag in each hand, Hope had a bouquet of flowers—she was big on aromatherapy—and I had Buddha. We were like a comfort brigade storming the castle to save the princess.

Marcel's shoulders stooped as he let us in with a sad smile. He looked tired, too. "So nice of you ladies to come. She's beside herself."

"I can only imagine," I replied. But the truth was, I couldn't imagine. If it were Buddha's fate resting in the hands of a killer, I wouldn't be able to put two sentences together, let alone a dinner party.

Talia's relief at our arrival was obvious as she hugged each of us in desperation. I could feel her tiny body trembling. "Come in, come in. Oh, those are beautiful." She took the bouquet of white lilies from Hope and breathed in their scent. "One of my favorite smells in the whole world. Reminds me of Easter, my mother's favorite holiday. She'd go all out with big family dinners and I'd always get a basket with so much chocolate, it'd take me months to eat it." Smiling at the memory, she took my hand and led me to the great room. The others filed in behind us. "Thank you all for coming. I feel so silly not wanting to be alone."

"Nonsense, no one should be alone at a time like this." Lulu handed her dish to Marcel. "For dessert."

"For our sanity," Beth Anne said, handing him the two bottles of wine.

He bowed slightly in acknowledgment and left with the items.

"So." Talia glanced at everyone as we got settled on the sofas. She was wearing a black silk pant outfit, her hair in a severe bun and her face scrubbed free of makeup. She looked so young and vulnerable. Her voice was high and tight, like she could snap at any minute. Her pale hands were trembling.

I had a flare up of rage toward whoever was causing her so much pain by killing Diggs and stealing Ginger.

Buddha sat between us, leaning on her leg. He must've sensed her fragile emotional state. She reached down absently and rubbed his head, like I imagined she'd done automatically to Ginger thousands of times. "Dinner will be ready in a bit but for now I need a distraction. Tell me about yourselves. Lulu, where are you from? You have such amazing bone structure."

"Oh, thank you. North Louisiana," Lulu said, smiling at the compliment. "Lincoln Parrish. My daddy was French-Irish and my mom is African-American."

"Ah, I should've guessed by your accent. One of the hardest to do in my opinion, so many different dialects. Well, besides Boston. No one ever gets that one right. That pie looks delicious. Did you make it yourself?"

"I did." She perked up noticeably. "One of my Grandma's recipes."

"Lulu is an amazing chef," I chimed in. "She owns The Gumbo Pot restaurant in Clearwater, where you'll get the best Creole food you've ever had in your life."

"Thanks, Elle." Lulu threw me a wilted smile. "Well, it's closed right now due to a lawsuit by some extremely rich and powerful crazy people. Sorry, that wasn't fair. Grief makes everyone crazy I guess. No matter our economic status."

"That sounds like an interesting story." Talia paused, watching Lulu silently, giving her space to talk.

Lulu didn't seem up to telling it though. "It's a long one. For another day maybe."

"Fair enough." Talia nodded, turning her attention to Hope. "Hope, what about you? Where are you from?"

Hope's sleek, brown bob swayed as she turned. "Oh, I grew up here. Well, more specifically in Clearwater. Elle and I are from the same neighborhood and have been best friends since the eighth grade. My husband, Ira Craft, and I have lived on Moon Key for a few years now, though."

Talia sat up a bit straighter, her eyes lighting up with recognition. "Oh, Dr. Craft, the plastic surgeon? Of course, I use him for touch-ups when I come here. He's just the best. A perfectionist really."

Hope and I shared a surprised glance. Ira apparently hadn't told Hope he'd done work on Talia. Client confidentiality, I guess.

Talia cocked her head. "And you, Beth Anne?"

Marcel appeared again with an opened bottle of wine and crystal glasses. He poured everyone a glass of the burgundy wine except Lulu, handing her a bottle of sparkling water instead.

Beth Anne took a mouthful of wine, swallowed and nodded her approval before answering. "Well, I come from a military family, so we traveled a lot. I met and married my first husband when I was twenty-three in Germany. He was a good guy, smart businessman too. We had a great time, a great life until he passed away ten years later of a heart attack. He was older than me. He left me millions so the next time I married a starving artist, my current husband and great guy, too, Carl."

"Any children?" Talia asked. Her face finally had some color as she got lost in our stories and her glass of wine. I awaited Beth Anne's answer with peeked curiosity. I'd always wanted to ask her this but had never wanted to seem nosey.

"Unfortunately, no." She tried to put on a brave face but the flash of pain in her eyes betrayed her. "I am apparently unable to have children." Lulu and I shared a sad glance. That must be hard. "But, I do have my Shih Tzu, Shakespeare. He's my baby." She paused and her gaze fell. "I'm so sorry. I shouldn't have…"

Talia held up her hand. "It's fine. I love to hear about other people's pets."

"Lulu's having a baby," I blurted out, trying to change the subject away from dogs and being awkward about it.

Lulu shot me an amused look. "I think everyone can tell."

"Actually I try never to assume," Talia smiled. "Congratulations. When are you due?"

"Oh, not until the end of April. Good thing, because I'll need time to figure out what this bundle of joy and I are going to do for food and shelter once I lose my restaurant." Her tone was joking, but I caught the sudden dampness in her eyes before she dropped her gaze.

"That won't happen," I said defiantly. But I knew it very well could. Lawyers with money behind them were pretty much invincible when it came to crushing the little guy. Or girl, in this case. Lulu couldn't afford to fight them. Plus Selene was not the type of woman to give up on revenge.

"So, no father in the picture?" Talia asked, her voice soft with empathy. "Or am I being too nosey?"

"No father and no, you're not being too nosey. It's just... that's another long story for another day." Lulu's hand shook as she lifted her water glass.

"I'm getting the feeling you've had a pretty interesting life," Talia said, tilting her head thoughtfully. "I'd love to hear about it. When you're ready to talk about it, of course."

Marcel entered the room, saving Lulu, and bowed slightly. "Dinner is ready Miss Hill."

"Thank you." Talia stood and held her hands together. A slim diamond bracelet caught the light as it slid down her wrist. Her smile was just as bright. "All right, ladies. You're about to experience the treat that is my chef's specialty. I hope you like seafood."

—◦୨୧◦—

We were all stuffed with delicious seafood paella, sipping dark roast coffee at the end of the meal when Talia suddenly glanced sheepishly at us. "I have something I want to get your advice on but... it can't leave this room unless it's something you think I should bring up to the police."

We all looked at each other and then nodded. She had our full attention.

Talia sighed. She rubbed her forehead nervously, closing her eyes. When she opened them, her resolve had stiffened. "Before I hired Diggs, I'd had another dog nanny named Rose. She'd been with me for four years and was also my personal assistant. I trusted her with my life. Until, well, she betrayed me... for money, of course." Anger darkened her expression for a moment. "She took secret photos of me." She lowered her head, her eyes hidden behind long, pale lashes. "Nude photos." Biting her lip, she raised her head and searched our faces with trepidation, for judgment, I assumed. When she saw none, she kept going. "I used to do yoga in the nude, just in the privacy of my own home, of course. But Rose took advantage of that and threatened to give the photos to the tabloids if I didn't give her a million dollars."

"What a horrible thing to do," Lulu gasped.

We all nodded in agreement.

"That's a terrible betrayal," I said quietly.

"What did you do?" Beth Anne asked.

Talia shrugged a slim shoulder. "I paid her, she erased the photos in front of me and I haven't heard from her since. It's been almost two years. But I've been thinking more and more lately, I don't think Sammy did this, and Rose is the only other person I can think of who would extort me for money. Plus the million dollar ransom? Seems like more than a coincidence, doesn't it? That it's the same amount."

"Could be," I said. "But it's a pretty round number."

"Nude yoga, huh? I'll have to try that." Beth Anne shot her a sympathetic grin.

Talia cracked a smile. "It's really freeing. Just make sure you're actually alone."

I forced myself to sit up straighter, feeling the weight of the food in my belly and Talia's dilemma in my heart. "I know it's embarrassing Talia, but I do think this is something you need to talk to Detective Vargas about. If nothing else just to rule Rose out. Do you have a photo of her? They could at least check the security footage at the ferry for any sign of her."

The other ladies nodded their agreement.

Talia groaned. "I know, you're right. I'll do it tomorrow."

"Besides Sammy and this Rose lady, do you think your neighbor, Nell, would take Ginger for revenge? And maybe the ransom request is just a smoke screen," I added.

Talia winced. "That poor woman. There were feathers all over my yard. I can't imagine why, but it seemed that someone wanted to set my dogs up to take the blame for killing her peacock. They didn't do it, of course. I never leave them unattended in the yard." She shook her head. "Anyway, I don't know. I don't know Nell well enough to say if she'd be that devious."

"Nell is a bit off her rocker," Hope said.

"Yeah, she is," Beth Anne agreed. "But murder and dognapping? She just doesn't seem the type. To kill or to need the money."

I set my empty coffee cup down. "Well, if the killer and the dognapper are two separate people, we should at least rule Nell out as having taken Ginger. If Ginger got scared off by the killer, she may've ended up in her yard, giving Nell the opportunity to snatch her up."

The women nodded, everyone getting lost in their own thoughts for a moment.

"Speaking of Sammy." Which we weren't, I'm not sure why I said that. "Has he called you back yet?"

Talia rested her chin in her hand. Half-moon shadows had formed under her eyes. "No, and it's not like him. I still can't imagine him killing Diggs or taking Ginger, though. He swore to me on Holly's grave that he had nothing to do with this."

Beth Anne was pressing leftover pie crumbs onto the plate with her fork. "So, you still trust his word, even after... you know... he cheated on you?"

Talia nodded and looked out the window thoughtfully.

I followed her gaze. The water was black with just a streak of moonlight across the surface.

Talia leaned back in her chair and crossed her arms. "I married Sammy because he's got a heart of gold, despite his profession. I lost him because of *my* profession. Even though I'm still angry about him leaving me, I understand why he did it. Being married to an actress is not for the faint of heart. I was gone a lot. And when I was here, it was hard for me to leave whatever character I was playing at the time behind. It becomes an obsession, really. To get every nuance of the character right, give her enough depth. Just the right amount of flaws. He never knew who he was coming home to. I don't blame him, really. Doesn't mean I don't want to rip the hussy's eyes out that he left me for." She winked at us, causing us to chuckle.

After a brief silence, Hope asked, "So, are you going to pay the ransom?"

"Yes." Talia shrugged. "What else can I do but pay it and pray that the kidnapper will keep his word and give me Ginger back alive."

"We still have two days," I said, with more conviction than I felt. "If we can figure out who has her, we can find her before Friday. We can't do anything about Sammy right now, or Rose for that matter, but what we can do is find a way to get into Nell's house and see if there's any sign of Ginger there."

Even Beth Anne was looking at me skeptically. That wasn't a good sign. She was always up for an adventure.

⸺⟨✦⟩⸺

When I got back to the bungalow, Devon was grinning at me from the kitchen.

"What?" I asked, half-distracted by the two excited dogs vying for my attention.

He came over and pulled Petey back so Buddha could get his kisses in. When I stood back up, he said, "I found Sammy and you're never going to believe who he's staying with."

NINE

"So how did you find him?" I asked, clutching a travel coffee mug as Devon navigated the Jeep down Moon Key Drive toward the Villas. It was early in the morning and the island was calm and still, except for a few white heron birds cruising the unlit skies.

He had his hand on my knee. I could feel the warmth through my black cotton yoga pants. "There's a workforce here, keeping the island running smoothly behind the scenes. The gardeners, the maids, the mechanics. People who maintain the golf course, the tennis courts, the common areas. A work force invisible to most."

I stared at his profile, the small uptick at the corner of his mouth. "But not to you?"

It became a full-blown smile. "Exactly."

I laughed. "So you have spies?"

He glanced at me. God I loved that little mischievous gleam in his eyes. "I have observant friends who are only making ten dollars an hour and enjoy a little compensation for their observation skills."

I smirked. "Like I said... spies."

Devon maneuvered his Jeep up to the resident side of the gate at Seaspray Villas. These were the two story Mediterranean-style condos sitting on the corner of

Moon Key between the west and south side mansions. He reached in the glovebox and pulled out a key card. As he held it up to the receiver and the gates creaked open, I said, "Well, isn't that handy. Courtesy of one of your spies?"

"My lips are sealed."

I leaned over and kissed him playfully. "I'm sure we can change that."

He chuckled, resisting my efforts at distraction, and pulled into a parking space.

We walked up to the door and my stomach clenched. I wasn't as worried about confronting Sammy as I was about coming face to face with my recently acquired nemesis. Every time fate has brought us together, she's made it a point to make sure I knew my place here on Moon Key... as the poor girl pretending I fit in with the uber-rich.

The blood rushed to my face as the door opened. There she stood in all her nude-except-for-a-skimpy-silk-nighty glory. Georgia Waters. *Femme fatale* southern style. She'd already swiped on lip gloss, so I knew she could've taken the time to put on a robe, too.

Classy.

"We're here to speak to Sammy," Devon said bluntly, thankfully saving me from trying to use my dry mouth.

Her blue eyes narrowed as she stared at me with a smug smile. "Still slumming it I see, Devon Burke, P.I." Then, when her remark elicited no response, with an exaggerated wave she added, "Come in."

My face still on fire, I carefully positioned myself behind Devon. He was my security wall, my shield against Georgia's merciless venom. I had felt sorry for Talia over Sammy's affair, now I felt sorry for Sammy. I'd personally pay to see Talia rip this woman's eyes out.

Not very yogi-like, Elle, I scolded myself. *What do men see in this she-witch?*

Unfortunately, at that moment, I raised my eyes from the floor and caught a glimpse of the yellow rose tattoo through the see-through lingerie, above her perfectly sculpted derrier. Guess that explained that.

She led us into the great room—blue velvet curtains framing the wall of windows, overstuffed butter-yellow leather furniture and gaudy gold and crystal accents. Then she sauntered over to place a hand on Devon's shoulder, guiding him to the sofa like he couldn't figure out not to sit on the low coffee table. My blood pressure spiked.

"Sit. I'll have Betsy make us some coffee. Someone looks a little tired." She turned her deep blue gaze on me. I didn't miss the fact that her nostrils flared with something that resembled disgust... or hatred as she clicked her tongue at me. "Those circles under your eyes are so unbecoming, Elle. You really should get more beauty sleep."

Devon shot me a sympathetic smile that said, "Don't let her get under your skin."

He didn't have to worry though. I was too frozen with humiliation to take her bait. And besides, she was already swishing her assets as she left us. I imagined her tripping in those fur lined heels and felt a little better.

We heard her call up the stairs. "Sammy darling, there's a detective here to speak to you." No mention of me. Good. The more invisible I am to her, the better.

"Just ignore her," Devon said, as I sat stiffly beside him, forcing myself not to enjoy the amazingly soft leather.

I fought back the tears, trying to take his advice. "I shouldn't have come," I said quietly.

He put a finger under my chin and made me look at him. "You're here because I need you here. By my side." He dropped a soft kiss on my lips and rubbed my hands in his. "Shake it off, darlin'."

Sammy swaggered down the stairs and into the great room. Luckily, he'd given us the courtesy of putting on pants, though apparently a shirt was too much to ask for.

Devon stood and held out his hand. "Devon Burke." I watched Devon's eyes narrow as Sammy took his hand. I could tell Sammy was squeezing harder than necessary. *A message?* Devon's jaw muscle twitched. He smiled at Sammy but it didn't reach his eyes.

Sammy plopped down like he owned the place, arms stretched out along the back of the matching leather loveseat. "How'd you find me?"

Devon didn't bother acknowledging his question. "You know the police are huntin' for you to answer a few questions."

Sammy licked his bottom lip and narrowed his gray eyes. His large shoulder muscles twitched under heavy tattoos. "And you're their dog, come to fetch me?"

Devon was quiet for a second, assessing the situation. "Look, this doesn't have to be adversarial. We both want the same thing. To find the fella holdin' Ginger for ransom and to put Diggs's killer behind bars where he belongs. Can you help us out with that?"

Sammy's expression went very still.

Georgia came back at that moment, thankfully with a white silk robe tied firmly in place, took one look at Sammy's face and slid down onto the loveseat beside him. Her French-manicured hand went to his knee.

"Sammy, what's wrong?" Her voice was different, soft and void of pretense.

Was it possible she actually cared about him and didn't just see him as another sugar daddy? Impossible. I didn't believe there was really a heart beating behind those saline implants.

Sammy ignored her, instead leaning forward and staring at Devon with a new, dangerous glint in his eyes. "What do you mean holding Ginger for ransom?"

Devon and I shared a glance, and I knew he was thinking the same thing I was. If Sammy did have something to do with the dognapping, he was one heck of an actor.

"Your ex-wife received a ransom note from a fella claiming to have Ginger and demanding a million dollars for her safe return."

His eyes darkened; his face turned to stone. "When is this exchange taking place?"

Devon hesitated. "Tomorrow night at midnight."

He jumped up and began to pace in front of us. "A million dollars? That's insane. She'll pay it, of course. That's how she is. Those dogs were her life. He better not hurt a hair on Ginger's head. I'll crush him when I find him." He was like a tiger in a cramped cage, raw power filling the room. I inched closer to Devon. Even Georgia sat back into the loveseat, having enough sense to leave the man to his rantings.

"Sammy, do you have any idea who did this?" Devon asked.

He shook his head as he rubbed his face and bald head with both hands. "No, I don't."

As I watched his anger, I got angry myself. Talia was the one suffering in all this. He should be thinking of her. I couldn't stop myself. "Why did you lie? That night you came over to Talia's... why did you tell her you'd just arrived on Moon Key when you'd actually arrived the night before? The night Diggs was killed." Defending Talia made me act braver than I felt.

At this, Georgia popped off the loveseat like something had bit her behind. Her voice shook with barely concealed rage aimed at Sammy. "You went to Talia's house?"

"Not now, Georgia," Sammy growled.

The maid walked in with a tray of china coffee cups. With a flick of her hand, Georgia flipped the tray into the air and the cups shattered on the tile floor in front of Sammy, splashing hot coffee on his shins.

"What the... " He glared at Georgia, who simply turned with a swish of her long blonde hair and left the room.

Sammy swore under his breath and then, with a shake of his head, addressed the startled maid. "Don't worry about that, Betsy. I'll clean it up. It was my fault."

Devon and I shared a look. "And why aren't you returning Talia's calls?" I asked.

He shot me an exasperated look. "You were just a witness to Georgia's temper. Returning my ex-wife's phone calls is akin to committing a crime in her book."

Sammy shook his head, looking defeated, as he squatted and began to pick up the larger pieces of broken china.

I couldn't believe it. This tough guy was actually afraid of Georgia. Sheesh.

He glanced up at us. A large vein bulged in the middle of his forehead. "Where is Talia supposed to drop off the ransom money anyway?"

"You'll have to talk to Talia about that," Devon said, after a moment of thought. "She should be the one to decide if she wants you involved."

"Didn't you just hear me say I can't talk to Talia?" Sammy glared at Devon. "You know this person is not going to give her Ginger back, even if she pays him. Why would he?"

"I know," Devon said, holding his gaze.

His shoulders fell in defeat. "Fine, I'll call her."

"How do you think they met? Sammy and Georgia?" I asked Devon as we drove back to the bungalow to pick up Buddha before my first doga class of the day.

"I guess here," he said, obviously distracted. "They used to vacation here together before the divorce. Guess Georgia got her hooks in him on Moon Key."

I noticed the tiny lines bunching up at the corner of his eye. "What are you thinking about?"

"I'm thinking about a way to follow that boat tomorrow night without bein' spotted. The problem is there won't be any boats on the water at that time of night, so tryin' to follow by boat would be too obvious."

"Ah." I watched a golf cart rolling over the dark green grass of the course to our right. Above it, the morning sky was a baby blue with mountains of white clouds. It looked like a tropical postcard. "What about some kind of tracker that we can put with the money?"

Devon rubbed his chin roughly. "I'm sure he'll look for that as soon as he gets the bag."

I tapped my foot against the floorboard. "So you don't believe the person who comes for the money will be an oblivious middle-man either?"

"I don't. Salma's right, the dognapper won't want anyone else involved in the exchange. Too risky."

I pushed my hair out of my face. "But, if everyone truly believes he's not going to give Ginger back alive anyway, what's the risk if he does find it? At least we might be able to get to him before he hurts Ginger if we know where he is."

Devon half-nodded, half-shrugged. "True."

I was getting excited, feeling like a plan was forming. "Do you think Salma would give us one?"

"No need. I've got a couple of luggage trackers that'll do the trick. We can even sew them into the bottom of the bag to make it harder for him to spot. But, you're forgetting one thing. You're going to have to talk Talia into letting us do this. It puts Ginger at risk and I don't think the argument 'he's going to kill her anyway' will be helpful."

"Yeah, you're right. Okay, say we can convince her that this is Ginger's only hope. How would we follow the tracker?"

Devon bit the inside of his cheek as he slowed for a light. "I'd have to wait off-island to see where the boat docks, hopefully it won't be too far of a drive. There is a possibility he could run up the coast, and it'd take me awhile to get there by car, but I'm betting the dognapper didn't venture too far from Moon Key."

"This could work. I'll talk to Talia tomorrow. You said before that Salma seems to think the person who has Ginger could be a different person than the one who killed Diggs. A crime of opportunity, if Ginger got scared, ran off and someone found her. If that were true, wouldn't it have to be someone on the island, and— besides the possibly of her neighbor, Nell, taking Ginger for revenge—I can't imagine any of the millionaire residents stealing Ginger for ransom money. But maybe a person working on the island?"

Devon thought about that for a moment. "Maybe. But I'm not so sure I agree with Salma. I think the murderer and dognapper may just be the same person and money was the motive to begin with. It usually is."

I reached over and squeezed his hand. I knew he was thinking about his parents' deaths. I sighed and changed the subject. "Do you think we should tell Talia that we know who Sammy's mistress is?"

Devon glanced at me. "Would *you* want to know?"

I thought about that. "Yeah... if it was anybody else but Georgia Waters."

TEN

I awoke Friday morning with my heart pounding and an immediate sense of dread. I scanned the room for any sign of my childhood dog, Angel, and breathed a little easier when her spirit wasn't perched on the end of our bed or staring at me from the doorway. I wasn't in danger at the moment, at least. That was more than I could say for Ginger. Today was the day. I had to talk Talia into letting us put the tracker in the ransom money tonight. How was I going to do that? I had no idea.

Hearing the shower running, I rolled over and draped an arm over Buddha. I tried to cuddle him but he squirmed happily and licked beneath my chin. Petey must've sensed we were awake and ran into the bedroom, leaping in the air and landing on us.

"All right," I giggled, fending off his long, wet tongue. "I'm up! Outside!" It was the only word that had the power to interrupt Petey's determined affection. He jumped down and scrambled to the sliding door. "Well, come on. You, too." I gave Buddha one last kiss on the snout and slid out of bed.

Reluctantly, he followed.

After letting the dogs out and feeding them, I started some scrambled eggs. By that time, Devon was out of the shower. We went over our plan for tonight during breakfast. My stomach was threatening to revolt, but I needed the energy so I forced the eggs down. My chest was already beginning to tighten. I thought about the anti-anxiety medication my doctor had prescribed. Maybe today would be a good day to take one. In the end, I decided I needed to be alert so I'd just have to deal with the anxiety another way.

We stood outside in the driveway, ready to part ways for the day. The salty air and endless expanse of blue-gray water spread out before us was a balm on my nerves. I turned from the view and slipped my arms around Devon. "Last day to change your mind about bringing Mom here tomorrow."

He laughed, tucking a stray wave of hair behind my ear. "It"ll be fine, don't worry."

Tilting my chin up, I searched his eyes for the strength I needed to get through this day. "Nothing is fine."

He kissed the tip of my nose. "It will be. I promise."

I knew he couldn't promise that. But at the moment, I'd take it.

—◦✧◦—

Lulu waddled in before my second class of the day. She'd been showing up a lot this past week. Even though she didn't have a dog, her changing body still benefited from the stretching and relaxing. I knew it was hard for her not to be working, and she seemed more and more depressed every day. That couldn't be good for the baby, either. I had to do something.

"Hey," she whispered as I hugged her, being mindful not to squash her growing belly. I could hear the suppressed tears in her voice.

"What's going on?" I asked, searching her face. "Is the baby all right?"

She blinked at the ceiling and shoved a finger under her bottom lashes like she was trying to dam up the tears. "The baby's fine. I just... I think I'm losing my mind."

I squeezed her shoulders. "Oh, Lulu, you need time to heal. Stop being so hard on yourself. You just went through a horrific ordeal. It'll take time. Here." I grabbed the dish of homemade raisin cookies off the shelf, courtesy of Nova, a maid here at the Pampered Pup. Devon had helped her sister beat a false murder charge and her family hadn't stopped bringing us food since. "Have one of these, guaranteed to make you feel better."

"Thanks, I'll try anything." She lifted an oversized cookie from beneath the Saran wrap.

Beth Anne and Violet made a beeline for us when they walked in and spotted Lulu staring at the cookie in her hand. "What's happened?" Beth Anne asked, wrapping an arm around Lulu's shoulder. Shakespeare gave Lulu's legs a good sniffing. "Did something happen?"

Lulu half-laughed as she lost control of her emotions and the tears spilled over and rolled down her face. "Now look what you did with all that caring. No, nothing new. I'm just falling apart." She bent over and gave Shakespeare a loving scratch with the hand not holding the cookie.

Beth Anne rubbed her back. "I'm sorry, sugar. Things will work themselves out, you'll see. All you need to worry about right now is keeping that baby fed and healthy, and we'll help you take care of the rest. You're not alone in this."

"That's right," Violet chimed in, her hand on her small hip. "Whatever you need, we're at your service. Heck, we don't have anything better to do. We'll start with lunch after class. How does that sound?"

Lulu wiped her eyes with the back of her hand and smiled sheepishly. "Y'all are the best. I'll be fine, just stupid baby hormones have me blabbering all over myself."

"Lunch it is," Beth Anne said firmly.

We all nodded in support. We all knew baby hormones weren't the whole story. Cooking at her restaurant had been Lulu's one joy in life. Now that had been taken away from her. I'm sure she felt unmoored and scared for her future. I remembered that feeling well.

Before I started class, I made a quick call to Talia. I was surprised when she answered the phone. She must not be sleeping at all. "Hey, Talia, it's Elle. How are you holding up?"

"I'm somewhere between numb and panicking." Her voice was shaky.

I bit my thumbnail. Don't screw this up, Elle. "I've got something I need to talk to you about before tonight. Can I stop by after my four o'clock class finishes?"

"Actually, I'll come to you. I need to get out of this house and need some company."

I glanced around at the full class, conversations buzzing, dogs sniffing each other. "Well, if you don't mind the crowd, the girls and I are having lunch here inside the Pampered Pup at Café Belle after class. Do you want to join us?"

"I'll be there."

⁓

Lulu, Beth Anne, Violet and I managed to score a window table at Café Belle as we waited for Talia to show. As the hostess led us through the crowded dining room, and around the large Banyan tree adorned with twinkling white lights, I noticed all the dogs at their owners' feet and hoped it wouldn't be too painful for Talia. I scolded myself for not being more sensitive to how dog-friendly this place was. Oh well, too late now.

Buddha and Shakespeare—already used to this routine and the treats that would be coming their way—plopped themselves down on the dog beds beside the chairs. But Ghost, Violet's emotionally needy Weimaraner, pressed his lean body up against Violet's chair, his brows twitching up and down as he eyed the crowded dining room.

"He'll be all right when the raw bone comes," she assured us, a loving smirk directed at her dog.

By the time we had our drinks ordered, a small woman in a pale green dress and dark, short-cropped hair was weaving her way through the tables toward us. She smiled as she approached. "Sorry I'm late."

We all gaped at her. "Talia?" I finally asked.

She slipped into the empty chair and slid off her sunglasses. The walk and hair was different, but there was no hiding those large blue eyes, smudges of dark circles beneath them, and doll-like face. "In the flesh," she quipped.

"Looks like you've perfected the art of hiding in plain sight." Beth Anne's gold eyes danced as she tilted her head with a grin. "Impressive."

"Well, it's a bit easier on a private island without the paparazzi jumping out at me from every corner. They tend to bring attention to me." She suddenly glanced down at the floor between her and Beth Anne. "Hello, Shakespeare. I love your pretty blue hair bow."

Beth Anne beamed at her dog as Talia bent over to scratch under his chin.

"He's so sweet." Talia's words caught in her throat, but she quickly recovered and turned her attention to Violet and then Ghost, who was still pressed against her. At least he wasn't shaking. "He doesn't like crowds I take it?"

Violet stroked his velvety ear. "Not really."

"I understand." Talia cocked her head. "His eyes are just the most stunning shade of blue. And so soulful. I sometimes wish dogs could talk. I bet they'd have so much to teach us."

"Oh, Lordy." Violet laughed, her green eyes glowing with good humor. "Maybe but I'm sure most of the conversation would be centered around bones and treats."

"Speaking of," Beth Anne chuckled.

The waiter approached and handed out the treats to our dogs. Then, noticing the addition to our table he said, "Can I get you a—" When Talia looked up at him, he seemed startled. To his credit, he recovered nicely. "A drink, ma'am?"

She smiled warmly, probably appreciating his discretion. "Sparkling water with lemon, please."

"Of course." He glanced down at the empty dog bed beside her and I held my breath, but he didn't say anything, thank heavens.

When he left, there was an uncomfortable silence.

Finally Violet broke the ice. "Talia I'm so sorry for what you're going through right now. I can't even imagine the stress of not knowing where your dog is."

"Thank you," she said. "Hopefully by tomorrow I'll have her back home."

Violet looked surprised. "Really? That's good news. Right?"

"We'll see," Talia said, not looking very hopeful. "I'm supposed to pay a ransom demand tonight and hope the person who has her keeps his word and returns her."

"I hope so, too." Violet's jade and gold bangle bracelet clanked on the table as she rested her forearms there and stared at Talia thoughtfully. "Do the police have any leads?"

Her gaze shifted to me. "That's one of the things I wanted to tell you, Elle. I called Detective Vargas this morning to let her know about Rose blackmailing me previously, which she said they would look into. But, she had also some news. They got what she called "touch DNA" off of Ginger's collar and it didn't match mine or Diggs's. They're getting a sample from Sammy today to rule him out, too." She clasped her hands together. "By the way, Detective Vargas told me you and Devon found Sammy, thanks. Where's he staying?"

My face warmed. "Oh, under his fake name like you said." I hated to lie to her, but I didn't think her frail state could take one more blow. And Georgia Waters would be a hefty sucker punch to any woman. "But that's good news about the DNA. You don't look very excited about it. Is there bad news, too?"

She loosened the dainty, silver chain around her neck with one slim finger. "Well, the DNA didn't match anyone in their local DNA database so they're trying to convince whoever they need to convince that it's eligible evidence to request a search of the national database."

Which takes time. Time we don't have.

Talia took a breath and forced a smile. "But enough about my problems, how are you feeling, Lulu?"

Lulu shrugged and tried to match her smile. "These baby hormones are really kicking my butt. I can't seem to shake the blues."

"Pregnancy isn't all glow and sunshine?" Empathy softened Talia's expression.

"No, not this one, anyway." Lulu laughed.

"Well, you did just go through a terrible ordeal," Violet said, resting a freckled hand on her arm. "You have to give yourself time to heal without pressure."

"Violet's right," Beth Anne said. "Time is a great healer." Then she flashed a grin. "And so is the chef's chocolate mousse."

"I'll second that," Violet chuckled.

We ordered our food and then it was time for me to bring up the elephant in the room. "Talia, Devon and I came up with a plan for tonight. But I need you to keep an open mind."

She was very still as I explained about the tracker, how Devon would wait on the mainland so he could follow the signal once the dognapper took the pay-off and started moving, and how this was the best shot at getting Ginger back.

Everyone was silent after I was done, waiting for her reply.

Finally she sighed. Her face had gone pale beneath the dark wig, like whipped-cream pale, but she met my gaze with determination. She wasn't as fragile as she looked. "What if the dognapper finds the tracker and tosses it before he gets back to where he's holding Ginger? The fact that we tried to track him would just make him angry and then he could… he could hurt her."

"That's a possibility," I said honestly. "We thought of that, so we're going to sew it into the bag beneath the money to make it harder to find if he's looking. But, if we don't try to track him, we have zero percent chance of finding out where he goes."

That is, if he even still has Ginger holed up somewhere alive.

The possibilities of her fate were many, but I was choosing to stay positive and believe she was still alive, and believe he'd return to where he was holding Ginger after he got the money. That's a lot of believing, I knew.

Talia picked up her water goblet and twirled it, letting the ice clink against the glass. "Okay, I trust you and Devon. Not so much myself lately. So, if you feel this is her best chance, we'll do it."

"We do." I sat back and felt my body relax under a flood of relief. One hurdle down.

"And we'll be glad to be some eyes on the mainland, too," Violet chimed in. "We can wait in the opposite direction of Devon in case the boat goes that way, tail him until Devon can catch up."

"Absolutely," Beth Anne said, her face lighting up at the thought of adventure.

"Whatever we can do, of course," Lulu agreed.

Talia's eyes began to shine as she looked at each of us with the first flicker of hope I'd seen from her since the night Ginger went missing. "This could work," she whispered. "This could really work."

"It can and it will. Okay, I don't know about you all but I'm starving." Violet glanced back at the kitchen, her mouth twisting. "Where in the world is our food?"

"They are taking an unusually long time," Beth Anne frowned. "Ah, there's Marco." She held up her hand and wiggled her fingers, her large diamond ring catching the light. Our waiter approached, looking apologetic. "What's going on with the kitchen today, Marco?"

The sweaty, balding man wrung his hands. "I do apologize, ladies. Our assistant chef has resigned only this morning without notice, and Chef Pierre is doing his best to keep up with orders. Your meals will of course be comped with our sincerest apologies."

"Poor Pierre," Violet said. Then she waved her hand. "That won't be necessary, Marco. We completely understand."

Sitting up straighter, I glanced at Lulu. I had a great idea. Maybe we could kill two birds with one stone at this lunch.

As the ladies talked, I called Marco over and kept my voice low. "I know Chef Pierre is slammed right now, but I think I have a solution for him. Can you just ask him to give me two minutes of his time?"

"No promises, but I will ask." Marco hustled back through the crowded tables to the kitchen.

"So, he's really as short as they say?" Violet was grinning at Talia, twirling a piece of her short red hair around her index finger. She had changed the subject to Matt Sterling, I'm sure to give Talia's nerves a break. It was a good idea. We all could use a breather.

Talia took a sip of her water. "Yep. Five-foot-six and very sensitive about it."

Our food arrived about fifteen minutes later with an overwhelmed, nervous Frenchman behind it in a white chef's hat. His face was beet-red but his dark brown eyes were soft. "I'm so sorry this took so long, ladies."

"Not to worry, Pierre." Beth Anne waved off his concern. "Your food is worth the wait."

"Thank you." He bowed. "Someone wanted to speak to me?"

"Yes." I held up my hand.

He hurried around to my side of the table. "What can I help you with?"

"Actually, I think I can help you." I held out my hand, gesturing to Lulu. "This is Lulu Dutrey, the owner of The Gumbo Pot, which is temporarily closed due to a silly lawsuit. And she needs to cook. You need a cook." I motioned between them, letting them put it together.

"Yes, of course, I know of Miss Dutrey. Hello. I've enjoyed many meals in your restaurant. Fabulous menu." He looked at her, his weariness shifting toward excitement. "You need work?"

She glanced at me, surprised. Then I could see the wheels turning in her mind, her excitement rising. "I do need to cook for my own sanity." She moved her gaze to Chef Pierre. "I'm really only good at Cajun though."

He grinned and held his hand over his heart. I could see his mind racing, then he snapped his fingers. "We can put Cajun on the menu, of course. Traditional Cajun food with a modern presentation. You like?"

Her face lit up. The radiant smile that had been absent lately suddenly appeared. "I like!"

He shook her hand vigorously. "You come in tomorrow morning. Eight a.m."

She nodded. "Thank you. I'll be here."

One problem solved. One big one to go.

ELEVEN

Fifteen minutes before midnight, Talia and I sat in her car in the parking lot of the guest marina. She was chewing on her lip, her eyes narrowed in the direction of the water. I wasn't sure which one of us was more nervous. The air conditioning was turned on full blast, but I still felt a rivet of sweat roll down my side.

"I should approach the boat alone," she said, straightening her shoulders.

"No way. What if his plan all along was to kidnap *you*?" I hadn't thought about that possibility before, but now that I had, my stomach flipped. What if this was her stalker's way of getting to her? "Besides, he didn't say anything about you having to be alone, so there's no reason to do that. Buddha and I are going with you and that's final."

She glanced in the backseat at Buddha and then her shoulders dropped. "Fine. Everyone's in place?"

I nodded, feeling my heartbeat ratchet up a few notches. "Devon's parked near the Clearwater Harbor Marina, which he thinks is the most likely place the boat will dock. But just in case the boat stops in Clearwater Beach, Beth Anne and Lulu are waiting there, between Priority and Municipal Marina. Violet and her boyfriend, Jarvis, are on the mainland about ten miles south in case all those guesses are wrong."

My phone vibrated, startling me. Maybe those anti-anxiety pills would've been a good idea after all. I checked the screen. "That's Devon. He has a clear signal on the tracker and says good luck."

A visible tremor ran through Talia. "Ready?"

The night air was chilly as we stepped out. It cooled the sweat from the back of my neck as we moved around to the back of the car. Talia popped the trunk open and we struggled to lift the heavy duffle bag.

"Who knew a million dollar's worth of hundred dollars bills could even fit in a duffle bag." I grunted as it landed on my toe. "Ouch."

Buddha made snuffing sounds as he sniffed the bag curiously.

"It's not as much money as you'd think." Talia bent at the knees and grabbed one handle.

I grabbed the other handle and we lifted together. I felt the strain in my lower back. "I beg to differ."

I didn't bother putting Buddha on a leash, since the marina was empty at this time of night. The only movement was the moored boats swaying gently on the black water. Only a sliver of waning moon hung in the sky. Peaceful really, if only we weren't scared out of our minds.

"There." I pointed to the end of the boat slips where a medium sized wedge-shaped boat with a flag sat idling. It wasn't under one of the tall lamps, so the boat floated in the shadows, and I couldn't see the color of the flag, but this had to be our guy.

We exchanged a worried look and then continued down the wooden walkway towards the boat. By the time we reached it, my arms were aching and my legs were jelly. I was also breathing hard from the stress.

A figure wearing a black jumpsuit and a ball cap pulled low over his eyes stood up. The boat rocked a bit. "Just leave it there," the figure commanded.

Talia dropped her side of the bag. Her breathing was coming in jagged breaths, too. I dropped mine. We were frozen. Not sure what to do next.

"Step back away from the bag," the dark figure called out.

I stepped back. A low growl rumbled in Buddha's chest. I reached down to grab his collar, and that's when all hell broke loose.

Something flew by us, shaking the wooden walkway. Buddha let out a surprised yelp.

A primordial yell pierced the night air as the boat rocked violently. Someone had leapt onto it and landed on top of the man in black. The two figures wrestled. There was cursing and grunting and more violent rocking.

"I'll kill you!" someone yelled.

"No!" Talia suddenly shouted. She stumbled toward the boat. "Stop it!"

"Talia, wait!" I called, lurching after her, still holding onto Buddha.

Just then a helicopter—I'd vaguely registered the sound of its approach—roared into position above us and flipped on a spotlight. Shielding our eyes, we all froze, staring up, trying to make sense of its presence here. Suddenly it shifted and I caught the letters on the side, "News 2." My heart sank.

"No, no, no." Forcing my legs to move, I grabbed Talia's arm. "We have to go."

To her credit, she had the presence of mind to take the bag of money. I grabbed the other handle to help her, and we hobbled as fast as we could back to the car, Buddha trotting behind us. We tossed it back in the trunk and took off out of the marina.

"Why? Why did he ruin everything?" Talia was sobbing, the stress released in uncontrollable tears as she drove us back to the safety of her mansion. "I wouldn't tell him where we were meeting. I told him I didn't want him to interfere!" she choked.

I twisted my body to check the sky above us. The helicopter was now swooping in our direction, its spotlight almost reaching us. *Drive faster,* I willed her. "Who was that?"

"Sammy," she said with venom. "He ruined everything." She steered through the open gates, pulled into the cover of the garage and shut off the engine. The garage door rumbled closed behind us. The heavy thump thump sound of the helicopter was above us. Falling forward, she let her forehead rest on the steering wheel. She sat there, her slight shoulders shaking.

There wasn't anything I could do or say to help, so I just stayed silent and let her cry it out. At least the helicopter was moving away.

My phone vibrated in my bag. I pulled it out. Devon. "Hey."

"The tracker's sayin' you're at Talia's house. What happened?"

I opened the car door to get some air. Buddha's hot breath on the side of my face was making me claustrophobic. My mind barely registered the black Hummer and old Corvette stashed in the pristine five car garage. "Sammy happened." Now that I had time to think about it, I got angry. "Talia says she didn't tell him where we were going, so he must've followed us. I'm sorry, we weren't looking for that."

I could hear Devon's attempt at staying calm but his voice was strained. "So the money hand off didn't happen?"

I rubbed my forehead, where a headache was threatening to bloom. "No. And worse than that. A news helicopter showed up."

"What? The press? How?"

I shook my head, lifting a hand helplessly. "Who knows."

Talia sat back up and wiped her damp face with the corner of her black, cashmere sweater. "I'll never get her back now," she said. Her arms went limp by her sides. She looked utterly defeated.

"We don't know that." I tried to be confident, but my words sounded hollow, even to my ears. I turned my attention back to the phone. "Can you gather everyone up and come to Talia's? I think she's going to need some support tonight."

"Be there as soon as we can."

⸺◦◦◦⸺

After sending Lulu home to get some sleep for the baby's sake, the rest of us stayed with Talia through the night, trying to keep her from sinking into a pit of despair.

Buddha had fallen asleep next to Ginger's bed, with his nose pressed into the side of it, as if it were too sacred to actually sleep in. Marcel kept a flow of thick, black coffee coming.

Talia clutched the green frog in her hand as we talked and tried to come up with a new plan. We decided there was nothing we could do besides wait and see what the dognapper's next move would be. By 5 a.m. we'd given up and turned on Channel 2 News.

I felt nauseous as we waited. After a commercial about a drug for constipation caused by other drugs, there it was: "Breaking News" video footage of Sammy and the boat driver wrestling in the rocking boat. Then Talia and I grabbing the duffel bag and struggling to get it back to the car.

I groaned.

The female newscaster spoke as the video replayed over again in the top right corner of the screen. "An anonymous tip turned into a scene ripped from the movies, as actress Talia Hill is seen here on the exclusive island of Moon Key, with an as-yet-unidentified female, in an alleged attempt to exchange a one million dollar ransom pay-off for the safe return of her beloved dog. Her dog nanny was reportedly murdered last Saturday, and her dog disappeared at that time. As you can see here..." the video paused and enlarged, giving viewers a still, grainy image of the two men in the boat. "One of the men appears to be Sammy Salazar, retired UFC champion fighter and ex-husband of Miss Hill."

"He doesn't look very retired," the other newscaster quipped.

"That he doesn't, Jim."

I glanced over at Talia. Her eyes were a cold blue fire, her jaw clenched tight.

"Well, it appears this exchange did not go as the dognapper planned. We can only hope this botched ransom exchange doesn't kill the chances of Ms. Hill getting her dog back unharmed. Clearwater police have declined to comment but asked that anyone with information about the murder of Jamie Diggs, or the whereabouts of Talia Hill's missing dog—a West Highland white terrier last seen wearing a pink collar—to call this hotline number they've set up." An 800 number began to scroll across the screen.

"Like they care," Talia growled, flicking off the TV. "An anonymous tip? No one knew where and when we were dropping off the ransom money besides us, Sammy... and the police."

Beth Anne had her legs curled up beneath her on the sofa. She yawned and then stretched her long arms over her head. "I don't think Sammy would've tipped them off, do you?"

I leaned forward and set down my empty coffee cup. "No, I don't. Maybe something good will come out of this, though. At least the public is alerted to Ginger being missing now and has a number to call." I turned to Devon. "Do you think there's a leak in the police department?"

He rubbed his palms on his jeans. "Don't know. But I'll find out. We'll go straight to the station after we get your ma settled in at home."

"Oh, yeah." My mood sank even further. "Today is the day, isn't it? I forgot." More like refused to acknowledge it. Guess it was time to face up to reality.

My mother was going to invade my perfectly blissful life, and I couldn't do anything about it.

I tried to tell myself that it'd give me a chance to spend time with her, that I would miss her when she was gone. The truth was, though, I didn't think I would. I couldn't imagine what I'd miss about her or our relationship, considering we never really had one. Besides me taking care of her. Then the guilt came. I had enabled her. I knew I had. I was partly responsible for her condition, her addiction. Pushing away the hot rush of shame, I stiffened my back. This was not helping Talia.

Devon's eyes were blood shot, his dark hair mussed from running his hands through it in frustration. He squeezed my knee and tried to give me an encouraging smile. Then he turned to the other sullen faces in the room. "Look, I think the best thing to do right now is keep up the investigation while we wait for the dognapper's next move. I'm sure he still wants the money, so I don't think we've heard the end of him. There's still hope, Talia."

Everyone agreed, trying to rally one last bit of encouragement for Talia, drawing from empty, exhausted reserves. It was time to start the day, and it was going to be a hard one to get through.

"Please try to get some sleep," I said to Talia at the door. "And call us as soon as you hear anything."

Her bottom lip trembled as she whispered, "I will."

I gave her hands one last squeeze and was greeted with a squeak from the green frog. The sound broke my already-cracked heart wide open.

TWELVE

I usually looked forward to Saturdays. Saturdays had become the day Devon and I played on the beach with the dogs, cooked delicious meals together, lounged around and just enjoyed each other's company. Today though, I dragged my weary sleep-deprived body and soul through the hospital corridors, clutching Devon's hand for strength. The tears were already prickling my eyes, and the anxiety was pushing my blood pressure up to audible levels in my ears. The antiseptic smell was churning my empty stomach into nausea.

I forced myself to breathe. I forced my mind to watch that breath expand my lungs and then let my lungs deflate slowly. I did this three times so, by the time we were walking into her room, I had my emotional storm somewhat under control.

"Hey, Mom. You ready to get out of here?" I busied myself gathering up her shoes and the plastic bag a nurse had stashed her belongings in, so I didn't have to make eye contact. "We're going to take you to Devon's place for a few days, to make sure you heal properly."

A dark-haired nurse was helping her sit up. "Will I have my own TV there?" Mom croaked through a dry throat.

"Of course, Ms. Pressley," Devon said, rolling the wheelchair closer to her bed. "And your own nurse to get you whatever you need." Devon and the nurse helped her slide off the bed and into the wheelchair. Her breathing was labored. Her face was pale, with an underlying yellow tinge. A bandage stuck out of her blouse below her neck.

"Guess money does buy everyone," she grunted.

I startled at her comment. *What did that mean? Does she know Devon's rich? How could she know that?* I shook it off. "Are you in much pain, Mom?"

"Well, they cut me open like a roasted pig, what'd you think?" A cough rattled her chest.

I gave the nurse a concerned look. "Is there anything we should be looking for as far as infection or anything else dangerous?"

She nodded. "Fever, any sign of redness or swelling around the incision area." She handed me a bag of medications. "There's a pain killer in there. Instructions are on the printout. Make sure she gets up and moves daily." She glanced at Mom and then gave me a wry smile. "Whether she wants to or not."

"Got it. Thanks."

Devon wheeled her around the bed, toward the door. "Here we go."

We got her settled in Devon's spare bedroom at home, putting up a gate at the hallway entrance to her room to keep the dogs out. Buddha already knew this wasn't a human who wanted his attention, so he steered clear when we came in the door. Petey, on the other hand, wanted nothing in the world more than to lick this newcomer's face. He spent the first ten minutes whining at the gate, dripping saliva on the tile from his panting tongue. I had half a mind to let him in. He eventually gave up though, went to find his bone and stretched out under the half-decorated Christmas tree to gnaw on it.

I tried to keep my tone cheery. "Devon and I have some things to take care of today, but your nurse will be here any minute and she'll stay with you tonight."

Mom clicked the TV channel changer repeatedly, not looking at me as she mumbled, "So you're just going to leave me here in this strange house. Got more important things to do than taking care of your mother, who just had open heart surgery. Typical."

I tucked the blanket under her feet, even though it suddenly felt very hot in here. "The nurse is much more equipped to deal with your needs. I'll get you some water. Be right back."

"It's not like you haven't left me before."

Ignoring her remark, I stepped out of the room and leaned against the wall. I focused on letting my anger go. *I will not let her get to me. I will not let her get to me.*

Once in the kitchen, I decided to make her a green smoothie. It would give her some much needed nutrition and besides... it would take longer than pouring a glass of water. I wasn't proud of my alterterior motive, but I already needed space.

"You doin' okay?" Devon wrapped his arms around me from behind as I shoved celery and kale violently into the Vitamix.

I relaxed into his body, letting him support me for a moment. "I'll be fine."

"You will be." His warm lips pressed against my neck, under my ear. I closed my eyes. "When the nurse arrives, let's head over to the police station."

He hugged me tighter against him. "Your wish is my command."

Just then the doorbell rang, followed by the dogs' barking. The nurse! I felt relief flood my body. "Saved by the bell."

Clearwater Police Station was busy today. As we waited in the crowded lobby for Detective Vargas, Sammy Salazar walked through the front doors, a gold-digging floozy on his arm in the shape of Georgia Waters.

I crossed my arms protectively across my stomach, wishing I'd done more than throw on my "I'll be Om for Christmas" t-shirt and pull my hair back in a ponytail.

Devon stiffened beside me.

They didn't spot us at first as they made their way over to the lady behind the bulletproof window. But since they had to wait, too, and there was nowhere to wait except the lobby, they headed straight toward us.

Georgia's eyes flashed like blue lightning when she spotted me. *Why did that woman hate me so much?* Then they narrowed and a secret smile touched her pink, glossy lips.

"Hello, Elle, Devon," she purred.

Devon ignored her, staring a hole through Sammy instead. "You know you put both Talia's and Elle's life in danger with that stunt you pulled last night. And destroyed any chance we had to follow the money back to Ginger."

He shrugged, his eyes equally full of rage. "I had to do something. We both know that scum is planning on taking Talia's money and running. We'll never see Ginger again. I couldn't just let him get away with it, without a fight."

Devon's jaw twitched. "I don't know that and neither do you. What are ya doing here anyhow?"

"I got a look at the boat driver. Not a great one. It was pretty dark and chaotic. But enough to try to make a go of it with a sketch artist."

Devon rocked back on his heels and stared at Sammy with growing intensity. "Any idea who tipped off the press about the exchange?"

I watched Sammy's expression carefully for any signs he was lying as he shook his head. "Nope."

Then I happened to catch Georgia out of the corner of my eye. She'd dropped her chin and was trying not to smile.

Oh. My. God. It was her! Why? Why would she do that?

Before my scrambled brain could come up with a motive, Detective Vargas charged through the door and approached us. Her dark gaze flicked around our group, assessing the situation and emotional climate. She missed nothing. "All of you come with me."

When we walked through the doors, she pointed to a conference room to our right. "Devon and Elle, wait for me in there. I'm just going to hand Mr. Salazar here over to the sketch artist."

Devon went to the folding table against the back wall and poured steaming coffee into a Styrofoam cup. "Want one?"

"No thanks." I lowered my weary bones into a chair and rubbed my arms. It was chilly in here. "Devon, I think it was Georgia who tipped off the press. Did you see the smirk on her face? I mean, it makes sense, right? Sammy probably told her about the exchange and where he was going, that he was going to follow us. Maybe she was mad that he was playing knight-in-shining-armor to his ex-wife. Maybe she wanted to mess up the ransom exchange or just couldn't resist the chance to hurt Talia."

He carried his coffee over and took the seat beside me, his finger tapping the side of the cup. After a few seconds he nodded. "A woman scorned. She does seem the type."

Anger exploded within me, threatening to lift me off the chair and catapult me down the hall to throttle Georgia Waters. "I don't understand how she can spend so much energy trying to destroy other people's lives."

"I know you don't." Devon leaned over and kissed my forehead tenderly. "That's one of the infinite reasons I love you."

I felt something shift within. Soften. The unexpected declaration of love in the middle of such hate and chaos stilled all the rage within me. It dissipated the storm so the important thing could shine through again. We're here to help Talia. I let go of my anger, felt it disperse and smiled a real smile. "You're so good for me, Devon Burke."

Detective Vargas entered the room with a growl, mumbling in Spanish under her breath.

Devon and I shared a concerned glance. "Everything all right?" I asked.

"Fine. Fine." She tugged on the ends of her black suit jacket roughly. "That woman just doesn't bring out the best in me."

I smiled sympathetically. Good to know I wasn't alone.

Salma slid into a chair across from us and rubbed the space between her eyebrows. "I just got to inform Mr. Salazar that we received his DNA results back this morning, and he is not a match for the touch DNA we pulled off the collar. That, along with Georgia giving him an alibi... and his behavior when he attacked the person who came to collect the ransom, suggests we can rule him out as a suspect."

"Where does that leave you suspect-wise?" Devon asked.

"Not in a good place. The neighbor, Nell Barnwell, was interviewed by Detective Farnsworth the night of the murder. I went back and reviewed his notes. He felt he had obviously woken her, and she was visibly shaken by the news."

"She could be just a good actress," Devon said, leaning back in the metal chair. "We're thinking even if Nell wasn't the one who killed Diggs, Ginger may've gotten scared and ended up in her yard. She could've used the opportunity to take Ginger for revenge."

"Then why the ransom demand?" Salma asked. "And what about the guy who actually showed up on the boat to collect it?"

"An accomplice?" Devon said, though he didn't look convinced.

I wasn't convinced, either. The theory seemed too forced.

With a growl of frustration, Salma stood and poured herself a cup of coffee. "We're missing a piece of the puzzle here, and I'm betting it's got something to do with the motivation for this crime."

"What about Talia's ex-nanny, Rose?" I asked.

"We're going to try and locate her today." She shook her head as she came back to the table. "But, according to Ms. Hill's description of her, she isn't tall enough to have struck the lethal blow. She could've had an accomplice, so we're not ruling her out yet. Ms. Hill also emailed us a photo of her. We'll go back over the security tapes and see if she entered Moon Key recently. She did have a pass that she never turned in."

"So, what we have so far is the killer is probably a left-handed male, six-foot, maybe an accomplice of someone else and has access to the island and a claw hammer. Not much to go on." Devon sighed.

"Not much," Salma agreed. "But one good thing came out of the news crew's ambush last night. Their footage is too grainy to get a clear image of the boat driver, but we did get a pretty clear image of the boat. It's a blue and white Cobalt Bowrider. Detective Farnsworth is going to take a photo around the local marinas today, see if anyone recognizes it." She softened. "Look, I'm sorry the ransom exchange didn't go as planned. But we both know she wouldn't have gotten Ginger back anyway. Probably just saved her a million dollars."

Devon's frustration flared. He gripped his coffee cup tighter as he glanced up at her through dark lashes. "We had a tracker in the bag. We could've at least followed the money to Ginger and maybe rescued her. Sammy ruined that chance."

"Oh." She shot us a sympathetic look. "I'm sorry. That was a good idea."

Devon sat up straighter and rubbed the back of his neck. "Anyway, we're hoping the dognapper will give Talia another chance, contact her again. I'm sure the fella still wants the money. Maybe if he sticks another note in her mailbox, someone will spot him." Devon's eyes widened and he clapped his hands together. "Why didn't we think of that before? Elle, call Talia and tell her to have Marcel keep an eye on the mailbox 'til we can get there."

Oh! Of course. There was no postage on the last ransom note, so someone had physically placed it in her mailbox, which meant they'd probably do it again if they hadn't given up on getting the money. I couldn't believe we didn't think about that before. Must be the sleep-deprivation. I called and left a message for Talia.

Devon pushed his chair back. "One more thing. The hand-off was obviously leaked to the press. We thought maybe the leak came from the department, and were planning on askin' you about that possibility, but now it seems likely it was Georgia Waters."

Salma's eyes darkened. "That woman is something else."

"Agreed." He stood up, but turned back for one more question. "Do you still think Diggs's assailtant and Ginger's dognapper could be two separate people?"

Salma gave a slight shrug. "My captain still thinks it's a possibility, so we can't rule it out. Though, the ransom demand does make the murder make more sense. Money is a solid motive. Which would mean you two need to be careful, because trying to find Ginger could lead you straight to the killer."

THIRTEEN

We headed back to Talia's to stake out the mailbox ourselves. Talia wasn't answering her phone. Hopefully, she was getting some much needed sleep. The alternative was going back to the bungalow to check on my mom. Hiding in Talia's yard seemed like the more bearable option. I trusted the nurse to have that situation under control, though we would have to go home eventually for the dogs' sakes.

The traffic was horrendous as usual during tourist season. It took us an hour and a half to make it back over the causeway and to the private ferry, which was the only way onto Moon Key. By the time we reached Talia's mansion and checked the mailbox, an unmarked, unstamped business envelope already sat inside.

Great. We're too late.

Glancing around, Devon swore under his breath.

I steepled my fingers in front of my mouth then dropped my hands. "Let's try to stay positive. This is a good thing. It means he hasn't given up on getting the money. And it was daylight this time. Maybe someone saw who put it there?"

We both looked around. It was a quiet day. The only movement was a couple of white ibises gliding by and the palm trees swaying in the breeze.

Devon took a few steps into the street. "There's no one around to ask."

Just then a whining motor noise caught our attention. We both turned as a red golf cart, sporting a red and white candy-striped awning, pulled out of Nell's gated drive.

Eva Gold.

"What about her?"

Devon nodded once. "Can't hurt to ask."

"Eva! Miss Gold!" I waved frantically as we hurried to stop her.

She eyed us impatiently as we approached, one hand resting lightly on the steering wheel, the other softly caressing the pug sitting on her lap.

"Hi, Eva, I'm Elle and this is Devon. Did you happen to see anyone hanging around Talia Hill's mailbox earlier?" I shaded my eyes from the sun and waited. It was hard to tell what Eva was thinking. Her eyes were covered by oversized, dark sunglasses.

She glanced behind us. "When I first arrived at Nell's house I did see Sunny Spillman's boy toy drive by in that garish yellow corvette. But, I didn't see him stop."

"Thanks, that could be helpful. No one else?" Devon asked, shifting his feet.

She cocked her head toward Devon, her expression staying neutral. "I've been inside Nell's for the last hour so I wouldn't know, sorry. What's this about?"

An hour? If she and Nell didn't really get along, and Nell opposed her during board decisions, what could they possibly have to talk about for an hour? I decided to come clean and be honest, hoping she would, too.

"There's a suspicious envelope in Talia's mailbox, and we think it might be related to Talia's missing dog. We're just trying to figure out who might have put it there."

Devon's phone vibrated in his pocket. He pulled it out and frowned. "Excuse me, ladies," he said, stepping away to answer it.

I decided to change tactics, since Eva didn't seem interested in helping us. Maybe flattery would work. "Thanks for your help, Eva." I glanced down at her pug. His shiny, black eyes were staring back at me. He had a gray muzzle, his tongue protruding from a flat face. "Cute dog, what's his name?"

"This is Peaches," she said, scratching him under the chin with her long, red nails. "He's been my companion for eleven years. Haven't you, precious?" She kissed the top of his head. "Don't know what I'd do without him."

It always amazed me how even the most uptight person's attitude changed when they talked about their pets. "I can imagine. I don't know what I'd do without my dog, either. Well, thanks again for your help." I turned to walk away.

"Elle," she called.

"Yes?" I said, turning back.

She seemed to be weighing her words carefully. "Just because I didn't see him stop doesn't mean he didn't circle back around after I went in. There's something... off about him. I wouldn't put it past him to be involved with Ms. Hill's missing dog somehow, especially after the ransom request. He's the male version of a gold-digger, if you know what I mean."

I nodded. "Thanks." Then I watched her drive off. Devon was just hanging up from his call, a distracted but intense look on his face. I pointed to his phone. "Who was that?"

His eyes shone bright blue in the sunlight as he looked up at me. "That was the owner of Brentwood Glass Studios in Miami returning my call. He confirmed the statue they created for Talia was made of safety glass, meant to shatter instead of break into sharp pieces upon impact. But he says that someone just fallin' into the statue, or the statue just fallin' over into a grassy area, would not be enough force to break the thick glass. It had to've been destroyed on purpose."

I bit the inside of my cheek, thinking. "Who would do that?"

His gaze moved to track Eva Gold's receding cart. "Talia had refused to remove the statue when Sunny Spillman told her to, remember? Maybe someone on the HOA board took it upon themselves to remove it for her. Maybe Diggs just went outside at the wrong time and caught 'em. That would explain why the murder weapon was a hammer."

I nodded, watching Eva turn the corner. "I hate to say it, but that actually makes sense. Except for the part where they took Ginger. If they were just there to destroy the statue, why take her? Surely none of the board members need the ransom money."

Devon shoved his phone back in his jeans pocket. "Then maybe Ginger did run off in the commotion and someone else saw an opportunity to make some money, grabbed her. Or she did end up in Nell's yard and Nell took her for revenge." He glanced back at Nell's house.

I sighed. There were too many what-ifs. "But then again, it still could've been Diggs's killer who took Ginger."

His eyes narrowed as he looked off in the distance. Then he snapped his fingers. "You know, one thing I've learned about rich people is they usually hire folks to do their dirty work. Say an HOA board member did decide to take the matter of Talia's statue into their own hands; it wouldn't be *their* hands that got dirty."

"They would've hired someone to take out the statue," I whispered. Yes, this felt like it made sense. "So, seven board members, seven suspects?"

Devon rubbed the back of his neck. "Maybe. We'll come back for the envelope. Let's go have a chat with Nell, since we know she's home."

As we made the trek down her driveway, I said, "Next we should go talk to Sunny Spillman's boyfriend. Eva said he's the male version of a gold-digger. If it was Sunny who'd decided to take care of the statue, he could've been her muscle. He could've destroyed the statue, then saw an opportunity to make some money by taking Ginger." Then again, maybe Eva was just trying to make trouble for Sunny. There was definitely bad blood between those two.

Devon knocked on the glass door with a frosted etching of a peacock. The woman was obsessed. I was surprised when Nell came to the door herself. *No butler?*

Her blue-gray eyes narrowed suspiciously as she opened the door and glared at us. "Yes?"

"Hi, Ms. Barnwell." Devon held out a hand. "Devon Burke."

She crossed her arms. "What do you want?"

"Just a word, ma'am." Devon dropped his hand. "We're trying to help your neighbor, Ms. Hill, track down her missing dog. There's a letter in her mailbox we believe is from the dognapper, and we're wondering if you saw anyone who looked suspicious in the area this morning?"

I didn't miss the slight smirk she was trying to smother when she asked, "She's really upset, huh?"

Devon's jaw muscle twitched. "Yes, ma'am."

She opened the door wider and stepped back. "Well, come on in and give me some details. Maybe I can help." She shifted her glance to me.

"I'm Elle Pressley," I said, stepping in behind Devon. I had to bite my tongue to keep from saying more. I knew she wasn't inviting us in to help Talia. She just wanted to hear all about how miserable Talia was.

She led us into a living room with oriental carpets covering the white marble floor and Queen Anne furniture scattered around the room—cushioned, wingback chairs, a large scroll desk and a buttoned, mahogany leather sofa and loveseat. An oil painting of Queen Elizabeth sat above the fireplace. Heavy, royal blue curtains with gold tassels hung across the floor to ceiling windows. Beyond the windows the sunlight glittered on the Bay waters beneath a cloudless sky. My gaze caught on a lone peacock pecking at the backyard grass.

"Something to drink?" she offered, taking a seat in one of the wingback chairs across from the sofa we'd settled into.

"No, thank you," we said in unison.

"Can't say I'm too upset to see that little rat-dog gone." She smirked at us. "She had another one, too. Together they slaughtered my poor peacock, Miss Penny. Good riddance, I say. Though, she must be beside herself, right?"

The way she leaned forward, eagerly awaiting our confirmation, didn't leave me feeling very warm and fuzzy towards her. "Allegedly slaughtered," I said.

"Ms. Barnwell." Devon jumped in as she narrowed her eyes at me. "Did you happen to spot anyone messin' about with Ms. Hill's mailbox today?"

She smoothed out her long gray skirt and shook her head. "I've been in the house all morning, sorry."

"We saw Eva Gold leaving. You two are friends then?" Devon asked.

She waved a large hand. "Friends? Lord no. We are adults, though, and can work together when we need to. For the good of the community."

"So it was board business you two were discussing today?" I asked.

She didn't answer me.

"The board had been pretty upset about the large glass statue Ms. Hill had put up, yeah?" Devon asked.

She lifted her chin into the air. "Nobody is above the rules. Not even a movie star, despite what she thought."

"Do you think anyone on the HOA board would've taken it upon themselves to destroy the glass dog?" Devon asked.

She looked startled. "Of course not. We're not savages, Mr. Burke." She thought for a moment. "Though, if you're saying that's what someone did, my bet would be on Eva. She doesn't let anything get in the way when she wants something. And she did want that statue gone. Her brother, Georgy, decorates the island for Christmas, you know. So she took it personally."

"Can I bother you to use your restroom?" I asked.

She waved a hand behind her. "Down the hall on your left."

"Thank you." While Devon continued his questioning, I hurried down the hall, checking as many rooms as I could for any sign of Ginger.

"Ginger," I called softly, as I hurried through a dining room, a massage room, a movie room, and a library. Eventually I made my way to the back of the house where there was a large kitchen. Nothing. No dog bowls, no food, no sign of white fur. I took the stairs two at a time and searched the upstairs rooms, praying to the universe I wouldn't run into a housekeeper.

By the time I raced back to the living room, I had to stop and catch my breath before I re-entered. I hoped she wouldn't notice how long I'd been gone.

"Well, thank you for your time," Devon said, standing as I reappeared.

"Anything?" he asked as we made our way back up the driveway.

"Nothing." I shook my head. "Except I didn't run into any maids or cooks or anyone else. Weird that she doesn't have any staff. Not that it means anything."

"She doesn't seem like the nicest person on the planet, but I'm not liking her for takin' Ginger. The fact that there's no sign of Ginger there, plus Salma saying the detective who interviewed her that night believed he'd woken her up, I think we can rule her out."

I watched a vulture making wide, lazy circles above us. "What about her throwing Eva Gold under the bus?"

Devon nodded and took out his cell phone. "I'll mention Eva Gold to Salma."

We walked in silence back to the mailbox. "All right. Here's the plan." He used the edge of his shirt to carefully lift the envelope out of the mailbox. "We give this to Talia, so she knows the dognapper has made contact, with instructions not to open it until Salma can get here. Meanwhile, we'll head over to have a chat with Sunny Spillman and see if her... friend's still there."

FOURTEEN

I felt bad. We'd left a frail Talia sitting on the sofa staring at the unopened envelope after we'd woken her from her first sleep in days. We didn't tell her about our new theory yet. I wasn't sure how much more her nerves could take. We'd run it by Salma when we saw her first. But right now, we were pulling around Sunny Spillman's circle drive. We parked right behind a bright yellow Corvette.

"He's still here," I said, climbing out of the Jeep.

Sunny opened the door herself, a confused look on her pale face. Cornflower blue eyes searched us suspiciously. In the crook of her arm rested a Maltese with a diamond collar and a pacifier in its mouth.

I stifled a giggle. Just when you thought you'd seen everything on Moon Key.

"May I help you?" She was soft-spoken and seemed to hold herself in check with good southern manners.

Devon did a double take on the dog and then composed himself. "Hi Ms. Spillman. My name's Devon and this is Elle. We're helping Talia Hill try and track down her missing dog and were wondering if we could have a chat with your... male friend. We think there's a chance he could help us. Is he available?"

She was nodding amicably, but there was something stiff about her smile. "Of course, anything we can do to help. I'm a huge dog lover and can't imagine what Miss Hill is going through. You can join me in my afternoon tea. I never miss tea time."

We followed her into the great room. "I'll go grab Valentino and have my butler bring us some tea. Make yourselves comfortable."

Her furniture looked like it came from an old haunted house. Victorian era, maybe, with all the ornate dark wood scroll work and hard, mustard yellow embroidered cushions. I wasn't sure it was possible to get comfortable in here. Instead I opted to check out the view through the floor to ceiling windows.

Unlike the other mansions I'd visited here on Moon Key, Sunny's was situated caddy-corner on the lot. So part of the Gulf was visible, but the main attraction was the huge banyan tree towering over a gorgeous beige bricked area beyond the pool. It was large enough for eight patio tables, with marshmallow-soft cushioned furniture beneath bamboo umbrellas, and some kind of guest or boathouse, surrounded by lush green scrub. A tropical paradise. She must have a lot of friends to need that many patio tables. Turning back to the grand room, I thought briefly about asking her if we could move our chat out there but, hopefully, we wouldn't be here that long.

I was pretty sure she was blushing as she walked back into the room followed by the younger man in an obvious state of post-shower dampness. The butler was close behind carrying a silver tea set on a tray.

"Valentino, this is Devon and Elle. They're trying to help Talia Hill find her stolen dog." I glanced at Devon to see if he'd caught the fact that she'd used the word *stolen* instead of *missing*, as Devon had, but his gaze was locked on Valentino.

Strolling over, Valentino shook Devon's hand then mine, which he held captive longer than necessary in a practiced manner of flirtation. I dropped my gaze uncomfortably.

He released me. "Of course. A terrible tragedy. I'm not sure how I can help." He slid onto the sofa beside Sunny, resting an arm comfortably around her. She shifted closer to him; her dog nestled on her lap, beady black eyes watching us from above the pacifier. After we'd taken a seat across from them, the butler handed us each a piping hot teacup. I breathed in the scent of mint and lemons.

"Thank you." Devon's tone was conversational. "We believe an envelope, connected to the dognapping, was left in Talia's mailbox sometime this mornin'. A witness saw you driving past her house, so we thought you might've by chance noticed someone near the mailbox or on the street? I know it's a long shot."

"I see." Valentino chewed on the inside of his cheek and closed his eyes. He shook his head slowly. Scooting to the edge of the loveseat, he sighed and picked up his teacup. "I'm trying to recall any cars or people in that area as I drove by. I think there were two golf carts and oh yes, a black Mercedes."

My heart sank. That wasn't very helpful. Those were a dime a dozen on the island. Just then, I noticed he was holding his teacup in his left hand. And he was about the right height for the killer. Maybe our hunch was right. The hair on my arms stood up. My chest tightened. I stood up abruptly.

Devon glanced at me, eyes narrowing with concern and then followed suit. "We appreciate you taking the time to speak with us."

"Yes, thank you." I walked over and shook both of their hands again to make sure. Yep, Valentino was left-handed. He was the right height, and he was seen in the vicinity of Talia's mailbox this morning. He also looked strong enough to kill Diggs with one blow to the head. *Was he the killer? Did Sunny put him up to smashing the statue?* She sure does seem like the type of woman who gets what she wants. I couldn't get out of there fast enough.

"He's definitely a suspect," Devon said, as we pulled up to the bungalow. We'd decided to go back home to feed the dogs while we waited for Salma to arrive at Talia's. It was going to take her awhile to get through the causeway traffic, even with a siren.

The dogs greeted us with epic tail-wagging at the door. I was really proud of Petey for not jumping on us, though. That had taken work, since he could've been in the Guinness Book of World Records for the most enthusiastic dog in the world.

"Good boy," I praised him as I let him give me chin kisses. "Okay, outside boys."

Devon had gone over and opened the sliding glass doors. It was turning out to be a beautiful day with temperatures hovering in the low seventies. I glanced around the living room but didn't see the nurse. "I'm just going to check on Mom. Be right out."

I peeked into the bedroom. The nurse was sitting beside Mom's bed, holding a bowl and spoon, her chin set in obvious frustration. A picture was flashing on the TV screen but it was muted.

"How's she doing?" I asked, though I could tell by the look the nurse shot me, things weren't going well.

The nurse placed the bowl on the night stand and stood up. "She's refusing to eat, and she needs something in her stomach before I can give her the medication. Maybe you can talk some sense into her." She raised her eyebrows at me as she left the room.

I took the seat she'd vacated and stared at Mom. She kept her eyes glued to the muted TV. I reached over and turned it off. "Mom, what's going on? Why won't you eat?"

She rolled her head toward me, her eyes flashing defensively. "I am not refusing to eat. I'm refusing to eat that tasteless liquid she's trying to pass off as soup. I need some real food."

I picked up the bowl. It looked like chicken noodle soup with homemade noodles and smelled delicious. My stomach cramped, reminding me it was lunch time.

"Mom, this is real food. This is what people eat. You've been living on nothing but sugar for so long, you're going to have to give your taste buds time to adjust to real food. Meanwhile, you're just going to have to eat what the nurse feeds you, so you can take your medication and recover. Your body needs proper fuel."

"Don't you lecture me, Elvis. You can just take me right on home if you're planning on treating me like a child." A coughing fit interrupted her and she winced, grabbing her chest. "It's my life and I'll eat what I darn well please."

I was too tired to point out that eating what she darn well pleased was the reason she was here in the first place. I stood up with the bowl. "Fine, what do you want to eat?"

"A peanut butter and jelly sandwich would be fine. That's not too hard, is it?"

The nurse was in the kitchen putting Saran Wrap over the glass bowl of leftover soup. She glanced up as I came in. "Any luck?"

"No." I sighed. "Not with the soup. I'm going to get her a sandwich and then you can give her the medication. I'm sorry she's so difficult."

She gave me a sympathetic smile. "Don't worry. I've dealt with grumpy patients before."

I pulled the almond butter out of the pantry. She wasn't going to be happy about the peanut butter substitute, but she'd get over it. "So, you'll stay?"

She laughed. "Yes, of course."

"Thanks." I unwrapped the whole wheat bread, knowing she'd throw a fit because it wasn't white bread, but it was all we had. Oh well, I don't think I've ever made her happy in my life anyway, why start now. When I was finished I held the plate out to the nurse. "Do you mind?" I just didn't have it in me to deal with her impending tantrum.

"It's what I'm here for," she said, seemingly regaining her good cheer during the break from my mother.

Devon was outside throwing a tennis ball for the dogs. I watched as Buddha ran after Petey. "His leg seems to be better. He's not limping at all. I guess those acupuncture and massage sessions are working."

Devon grinned at me. "Or he was faking to get out of the daily runs you were making him go on."

I laughed at first. But then I crossed my arms and stared at my dog, watching him happily roll around on his back in the grass. My eyes narrowed. Thinking back, I did only notice him limping when I'd get my bike out. "He couldn't be that... calculating. Could he?"

Devon laughed as he chucked the ball. "Indeed, I think he could." His phone vibrated in his jean's pocket. Pulling it out and glancing at the screen he said, "Salma's there. Time to go."

I brought Buddha with me. I wasn't used to spending so much time without him, and I needed him for emotional support. I was getting nervous about what the letter would say this time. What if he'd hurt Ginger as revenge for the botched ransom exchange?

No, don't even go there, Elle.

The short drive felt like an eternity. We were both silent, lost in thought. Devon pulled behind Salma's car and we jumped out, anxious to end our speculation about the envelope.

Salma and the officer who'd been with her before, were standing in front of the coffee table. Talia was still sitting on the sofa in the same position we'd left her in.

She jumped up to greet us with a hug, though, her eyes wet with new hope. "He's sent a photo of Ginger to prove she's still alive. He still wants the money," she said breathlessly, with obvious relief.

"That's great news, Talia." I hugged her again. "See, we're going to get her back." Then Devon and I went to have a look at the plastic encased letter Salma was holding.

My heart clenched with both joy and anger. There was Ginger. Alive. She was stretched out in grass, her head resting between her paws, her eyes turned away from whoever was taking the picture. She had a new collar on, gold with silver rivets. It glinted in the sun.

"She looks good, Talia," I managed through the storm of emotions I was feeling. "Looks like she's being taken care of." There was a newspaper lying in front of her. The date was circled in red marker. It was yesterday's paper.

"That's the Moon Key Gazette." Devon sounded surprised. "That means she's still on the island."

"Possibly. Would they be that stupid to give us such an obvious clue?" Salma answered. She handed Devon the second letter she'd been holding beneath the photo.

We read it together:

I realize it's not your fault someone leaked the last drop off to the press. So, I'm going to give you one more chance to get your dog back. I've sent the photo to prove I'm not playing games. She will be returned to you alive once I have the money. This time there will be a series of instructions for you to follow. The first will be in place at eleven p.m. tomorrow evening at the Clearwater Church of the Nazarene on Main Street. There'll be a brick on the back east corner with instructions underneath it. NO police.

"Screw that. This time I'm going to be there," Salma said. "Whether my captain likes it or not. I'll go as a concerned citizen. With a gun."

"No, please," Talia said, distress filling her eyes. "I really think we should just do what he says. I truly believe he'll give her back to me unharmed, and I don't want to jeopardize that."

Salma's mouth twisted in frustration, but she said, "Okay. Your dog, your call."

Devon was thinking out loud when he mumbled, "I'll ask around my sources, see if anyone has given their staff time off. If one of the board members is involved, and Ginger's still on Moon Key, then they'd need to hide her from the staff."

"Board members?" Salma asked.

Devon rubbed his stubble. "I've not had a chance to fill you in yet, but I called the glass company that made the statue of Holly. They confirmed it was safety glass, meant to shatter, but just being knocked over wouldn't have done it. Someone would've had to smash it on purpose. The only folks we know of who didn't want the statue up are the HOA board members. They could've paid someone to destroy it. I'm thinking maybe Diggs surprised the vandal, and he attacked Diggs with the hammer he was using. That could be the missing motivation we're looking for. Not Diggs or Ginger, but that statue."

Salma stared at the floor for a moment and then back at Devon. "Wouldn't the HOA just have asked Ms. Hill to remove it? Why go to all the trouble of destroying it?"

Devon's hands were perched on his hips. He nodded. "They did ask her to remove it. She was paying a thousand dollar fine every day it was left up."

Salma looked surprised as she glanced at Talia. "That true?"

Talia nodded.

"Well, that actually makes sense then. The hammer was a weapon of opportunity."

Talia was staring at them in horror. "Diggs was possibly killed because of my statue?"

I went and sat down beside Talia. "Only one person is responsible for his death and that's the person who killed him."

"She's right, Talia. One more thing," Devon said. "We just spoke with Sunny Spillman, a board member, and her young boyfriend, Valentino, who was spotted driving on this street this morning. He's a strapping lad, the right height and is left-handed."

"Though, he was pointed out to us by Eva Gold, the HOA president, who I wouldn't discount as a suspect, either. She's got a history of violent altercations with residents and doesn't take kindly to not getting her way. My friend, Violet—" I stopped, realizing I'd just called her 'my friend.' But yes, I did consider her a friend, didn't I? Not just a doga client. I felt warmth bloom in my chest. "Violet told me she suspects Eva was the one who got rid of Nell's peacock and framed Talia's dogs. Oh and I also overheard Eva blackmailing Sunny to get her to change her vote at a board meeting."

Salma blinked and shook her head a little. "Blackmailing her with what?"

I shrugged. "Don't know."

"Do you have the addresses of these two board members?" Salma asked, taking out her notepad and pen and handing them to Devon.

Devon clicked the pen. "I don't know the house numbers but I'll draw you a map."

"Thanks," Salma said. "That gives us somewhere to start. I'll begin by questioning Eva Gold, Sunny Spillman, and her boyfriend; see if they all have an alibi for that night. If they don't, I can try to get a warrant to search their property. And maybe Sunny Spillman's boyfriend will cooperate and also give us a DNA sample to compare to the touch DNA off the collar. While we don't have a match, we do know it's from a male." She turned to the officer. "We have the kit in the car, right?"

He nodded. "Yes ma'am."

"Or maybe he won't cooperate and we have a solid suspect," Devon added, handing her pen and notepad back to her. "Either way, keep me in the loop."

"You, too." She looked down at Talia. "Ms. Hill, I sincerely hope all goes well and you get Ginger back safe and sound."

Talia's lip trembled as she said, "Thank you."

I glanced over at Ginger's bed, where Buddha lay sulking beside it. I shouldn't have done that, the tears sprung up. I had to be strong for Talia.

After Salma and the officer left, Talia said, "So what's the plan for tomorrow night? Think you can follow my car without him spotting you?"

"I won't necessarily need to follow you as much as stay around the area so I can follow the money. We can keep in touch through text, and the tracker in the duffel bag'll tell me where you are. The important thing is that I'm close enough to stay on the money trial. This'll actually be easier to do in town so that's a positive thing for us."

Talia's phone buzzed on the end table beside her. Picking it up, she frowned. "It's my publicist. She's driving me crazy. I don't give two hoots about my image right now and she just doesn't get that." Tossing the phone back on the table unanswered, she leaned back into the couch. "Before you came, Salma told me they'd ruled out Rose. She's apparently now living in Germany. Living pretty well, too." Anger flashed for a second then dissipated in the sadness.

"Well, that's good," I said. "The more possible suspects we can rule out, the closer we get to the truth."

"That's very optimistic of you, Elle." She did smile then, though it quickly disappeared. "Sunny Spillman was pretty angry after she'd confronted me about the statue and I'd told her it was staying right where it was," she said, thoughtfully. "I can't imagine her being the one responsible for Diggs's death, though."

I pulled my hair off my neck. It was getting warm in here. "No, but Valentino? Maybe."

FIFTEEN

Sunday afternoon I had to attend the annual Christmas party at the Pampered Pup Resort and Spa. It was mandatory for staff, as Rita thought it'd be a good opportunity to sell our services to the guests. A lot of them were surprised to find out we offered pet acupuncture, mud baths and other spa treatments, even dog psychotherapy. Lord knows what went on in there. Do dogs even remember their mothers?

Rita had also roped Devon into taking candid photos at the event, since he'd done such a good job at the Halloween party. So, we were both indentured servants today.

I'd decided on a simple green, long-sleeved satin dress and wore my wavy auburn hair down around my shoulders. Devon wore a white button-down shirt with black slacks and a red tie. We were both anxious and not in the mood for a party. Tonight would be the second attempt at a ransom drop-off. And the last. If this didn't work, there was no hope of getting Ginger back.

We walked into the lobby. I had to give Rita credit for the transformation. The giant Christmas tree had been set up for a few weeks, but she'd added a long bar to the left where a line of people currently waited for drinks. There was also a stage in the corner with a band playing live Christmas music. Hundreds of strings of multicolored Christmas lights crisscrossed the ceiling, along with twinkling white Christmas lights outlining the portraits of Priscilla Moon's three Yorkies behind the front desk.

"Guess I'll just wander around and get some shots," Devon said, holding up his camera with a playful smirk.

"Have fun." I grinned, squeezing his hand. "I'll catch up with you later."

Rita spotted me and made a beeline. She was wearing a red sequined cocktail dress and Santa hat. "Elle!" She stood in front of me breathless and then glanced behind me, disappointment surfacing.

"Something wrong?" I asked.

"Well." She dropped her gaze sheepishly, then gave me a shrug. "I was hoping you'd convince Talia Hill to come today. I heard you were giving her private doga lessons and thought you'd mention the party."

I should've known. Gossip was a sport on this island. "Sorry, she's kind of busy... you know, and not in the mood for parties considering the situation with her dog missing and all."

"Right." She waved off her disappointment. "Of course. Well, anyway, I've had some coupons printed up for our services, offering the first one of each free. If you want to grab some at the counter and just mingle, hand them out, explain what your doga classes are, that sort of thing."

"Coupons?" I smirked. "Does that work with this crowd?"

She smiled. "You'd be surprised how well. Everyone likes a bargain." She began to walk away and then turned back. "And don't forget to grab a Santa hat!"

I went to the desk and grabbed a handful of coupons and our required Santa hat, shaking my head. These people paid cash for six-figure cars, and they were going to be happy about a free acupuncture session for their dog? I shrugged and went to mingle.

As I adjusted the scratchy hat on my head I glanced around. The first person I spotted, and recognized, was Eva Gold. She was wearing a black pantsuit accented with a thick gold necklace. Her short, dark hair was slicked back. She was deep in conversation with Gwen, who I recognized from my doga class. Gwen had her little wire-haired terrier, Gilly, cradled in her arms.

Perfect. If I could get Eva into my doga class, I'm sure I could get to know more about her. If not me, than maybe Beth Anne could. She was great at getting people to spill their secrets.

"Hi, ladies," I said, plastering on my biggest smile. "Sorry to interrupt your conversation. Hi, Gwen." I reached over and gave Gilly a scratch under the ear. Her tongue caught my wrist and I chuckled. "Missed you and Gilly in class this week."

"Yeah." Gwen rolled her eyes. "My in-laws are staying with us for a few weeks. They're stressing me out. I'm really going to need your class when they leave. Speaking of, I was just telling Eva she should come with Peaches."

I turned my attention to Eva. "What a great idea. We'd love to have you both. In fact, here's a coupon for your first class free. No risk." I handed it to her, noting she took it with her left hand. Also, standing next to her, I realized what a tall woman she was. I'd only seen her sitting.

She glanced down at Peaches skeptically. The pug was sprawled out on the floor like a fat little rug. "Doggie yoga, huh? Might do him some good."

"I also do private lessons in your home, if you prefer that," I said, hoping that wouldn't make her suspicious. Maybe if I could get inside her mansion I could find a way to snoop around for any signs of Ginger.

Her expression seemed to shut down. *Or was that my imagination?* She didn't have the friendliest face to begin with.

"Did you have any luck with talking to Sunny Spillman's boy toy yesterday?" Eva asked, a bit of venom seeping through.

What was that? Anger? Jealously? "No," I answered. "I mean, we did speak with him, but he didn't see anyone put the note in Talia's mailbox."

She nodded with a sly half-smile, her dark eyes suddenly glittering. "And I don't suppose he'd confess to doing it himself."

"Talia Hill?" Gwen put a hand on her chest, her cherry red polish matched her silk top perfectly. "Isn't that awful what happened. I can't believe someone murdered her dog nanny and stole her dog. For ransom, no less. You'd think Moon Key would be safe enough that things like that wouldn't happen here."

I stared at Eva. "Yes. You'd think."

Her comeback was interrupted by the DJ. "All right, ladies and gentlemen. It's time for the first raffle of the day so get out your tickets. This is for a chance to win a genuine Michelle Marley designer, diamond-studded collar for your canine friend." He read off the number.

I watched in fascination as women dripping in diamonds and other jewels dug in their designer purses for raffle tickets. Humans were weird. I excused myself and went to look for Devon.

I found him having a beer with a man dressed in a Santa suit, who apparently was on break. I stole him away from his new friend. "How's it going? Have you seen Sunny or any of the other board members here?"

"Look at you. Nice hat, Santa." He kissed me and then stepped back and lifted his camera. "Smile."

I rolled my eyes. He knew I hated having my picture taken. And I knew he wouldn't give up, so I gave him my best cheesy smile. He snapped the photo and grinned at me, though I was looking at him through tiny white spots from the flash.

I blinked my eyes. "So, have you? Seen any of the other board members?"

He shook his head, adjusting his camera on his shoulder. "Just Eva Gold."

I shifted on my feet and glanced over my shoulder. "Yeah, I already talked to her. Offered to come to her house to give her and Peaches a doga lesson. She didn't seem too excited about the idea."

"Elle." Devon gave me his serious expression. "You're not to be putting yourself in situations where you're alone with a possible killer."

I frowned. "You really think she's capable of murder?"

"I don't know the woman enough to say one way or another. Though, I'm inclined to say yes considering the stories we've heard about her tendencies toward violence. But that's not the point. The point is we don't know. So, you going to her house alone is a bad idea."

"Fine." I pouted.

He planted a kiss on my pouty lips. "Have to go earn my keep."

"You know you're working for free," I called after him.

I spent the next hour giving out the coupons, mingling and talking. It was exhausting, and I was starting to get really nervous about the ransom drop-off tonight. Just as I was wondering if we could sneak out early, I recognized Jata, the tall board member with shoulder-length dark hair and an accent that sounded Middle-Eastern.

I watched as she greeted Eva and then walked over to the line at the bar. I crossed the room to stand behind her. Her perfume was strong and spicy, like cloves.

"Are you enjoying the party," I asked as an icebreaker, even though I knew she'd just arrived. Zero points for imagination, I know.

Her smile, which appeared as she glanced at my Santa hat, was painted tangerine orange beneath dark, kohl-lined eyes. "Not yet. I've just arrived. It looks lovely, though."

I held out my hand. "I'm Elle. I recognize you from the HOA board meeting. I teach doggie-yoga here. Do you have a dog?"

She laughed good-naturedly. "I do, two actually. They're Scottish Terriers."

I nodded. "Terriers are very popular dogs. Did you hear about Talia Hill's West Highland terrier being stolen?" Not a very smooth transition, but it was all I had.

Her hand went to her neck. I noticed her nails were painted the same bright orange. "I did. She must be going out of her mind with worry. I saw on the news her dog nanny was killed, also. Just horrible."

"Yes." I glanced around and moved closer, dropping my voice. "One of the theories the police are batting around is that someone was actually there that night to destroy Talia's glass dog statue, and Diggs just happened to catch them. You know, in the wrong place at the wrong time." I watched her face for any signs she knew anything about it.

Her eyes widened. Her hand spasmed around her diamond necklace. "Someone went there to vandalize the dog statue?"

"Yes. Have any ideas who would do that?" I kept my gaze locked with hers.

She glanced sharply across the room. "Well, it wasn't authorized and Eva was pretty upset about it. Her brother's business decorates for the island, you know." I nodded. "But, no, I can't see her sneaking out in the middle of the night to destroy it." Despite her denial, the corners of her eyes were still creased with suspicion or worry.

We moved up as the line shortened. "Is there anyone else on the board you could see doing that?"

She tapped her lip with one nail. "No, no one."

"What about Nell?" I asked.

She shook her head. "Definitely not Nell. She could've cared less about that statue." Then she thought for a moment. "Talia's dog, on the other hand, she didn't care for."

We were almost at the front of the line now. "Do you think that if someone else smashed the statue, and Talia's dog ran away from the commotion, Nell could possibly have used that opportunity to take the dog?"

She smiled dismissively. "Well, I don't see what she would gain from doing that. Besides maybe upsetting Talia. But, that seems a stretch."

I nodded in agreement. But, in my head I was thinking what she had to gain was a million dollars. Still, there was no sign of Ginger at Nell's house. We should probably be concentrating on learning more about Eva.

SIXTEEN

That evening, we were back in Talia's car, heading toward the Clearwater church on Main Street with the million dollar duffle bag. Buddha was sprawled out on the back seat, unimpressed with me waking him up so late for an outing. I felt better when he was with me though, so he'd just have to suck it up.

Talia had put on a short brown wig. It made her look almost human, instead of like a silver screen goddess, as long as you didn't get a good look at her face.

"How are you holding up?" I asked her.

"I just feel numb," she answered, after a deep breath.

The GPS app interrupted any reply, probably for the better. There was really nothing I could say. "In a quarter mile, turn left on Duncan Street."

My phone buzzed. "It's Devon," I said. "He's just letting us know he's in place and has a clear signal from the duffel bag."

"In fifty feet turn left on Main Street. Your destination will be on the right."

"Here we go," Talia whispered, pulling into the church parking lot. She circled the large, stone building until she came to the back and parked. "Be right back."

I nodded anxiously, scanning the area for any signs of movement. There was only one street light in front of the church, so this back area was dark. "Hurry." I watched as she kneeled by the door and then ran quickly back to the car.

She was breathing hard when she slid back into the driver's seat and pulled the door shut. "Here it is."

Using my phone light, we read the instructions typed on the plain white sheet of paper.

"I'll text this to Devon." I took a photo and sent it to Devon.

We were off again, this time toward Tripp's, a small diner on the other side of town. This went on for an hour, ping-ponging from one side of Clearwater to the other until tears of frustration ran down Talia's face. "What kind of game is he playing?"

"Stay strong," I said. "He just wants to make sure we're not being followed. There can't be many more places. He does want the money after all."

Finally, at the marina the instructions were for her to place the bag at the end of the dock and leave the area immediately.

"Oh no," I whispered, my heart sinking. "He's still using a boat for the pick-up."

Talia's hands cupped her mouth. She stared out at the hundreds of boats docked there in the dark. Her hands fell into her lap and she moaned. Her expression was a mixture of frustration and anger. "He could be waiting in any one of those boats. Which means Devon won't be able to follow him in a car."

Panicked, I called Devon's phone. When he picked up I blurted out. "We have to leave the money on the end of the dock. He's still using a boat. What should we do?"

There was silence and then cursing. "Leave the money. It's still Ginger's best chance. If he sticks close to the shoreline, maybe the tracker will stay in range."

"Okay." I hung up and glanced over at Talia. "We stick with the plan."

Talia shut off the car.

Once again, each of us grabbed a side of the heavy bag and lugged it out of the trunk. I let Buddha snooze in the back seat this time. As we hobbled along, I scanned the dark skies but saw no signs of a helicopter as we dropped the bag on the end of the dock and made our way back to the car.

"Do you think he's watching us?" I whispered. The hairs on my neck were standing up, and I had the urge to run.

"Most likely." Talia's voice sounded flat, defeated. But then she stopped, her head jerking up. She turned toward the dock and screamed. "Now give me back my dog!"

Fighting back tears of my own, I wrapped a protective arm around her and led her quickly back to the car.

By the time we'd arrived back at Talia's house, we'd received news from Devon. It was not good news. The signal from the tracker had stopped in the Gulf and then disappeared. The dognapper must've found it or just switched bags and thrown ours overboard.

Now all we could do was hope he'd keep his promise and return Ginger.

⌁

Monday morning Devon was waiting for me in the kitchen after I'd checked on Mom. His laptop bag was slung over his shoulder and he had a far-off look in his eyes.

"What's up?" I said, coming to stand in front of him.

Rubbing my arms gently, he kissed me. "I'm going to be out today. I've got something to take care of that's a few hours drive. I'll be home really late so don't wait up, but text me if there's any news from Talia."

"Oh." I wrapped my arms tighter around his waist. I wasn't looking forward to an evening without him, especially with all the anxiety surrounding the situation with Talia. "This isn't anything dangerous you're doing, is it?" I still worried about him investigating his parents' case. There were some shady characters involved.

"It's not, don't worry. Just some other investigative work." He pulled me into him. I let my head rest on his chest, breathing in his scent. Then we said goodbye in the driveway and went our separate ways. It was going to be a long day.

⁕

I sat cross-legged on the wood floor at the front of the doga room with Buddha sprawled out in front of me. "Good morning, everyone." I waited for the ladies to quiet their conversations and get settled on their mats before continuing. "I'm sure you've noticed your dogs picking up on the more hectic holiday energy lately."

In the back, a yellow Lab barked and pounced on her owner. A light chuckle rolled through the class.

"Thank you for proving my point, Godiva," I said, addressing the dog with a grin. "I think today we'll turn down the lights and do a more restorative session. If you haven't done so, please go get three blankets each from the storage closet."

While they did that, I picked my way through the mats to retrieve my jacket. Rita must've turned the air conditioning on in anticipation of the higher temps today. It was supposed to be in the low eighties but, unfortunately, this morning it was still chilly. As I repositioned myself on my mat, I zipped up my jacket and shoved my hands in the pockets. That's when my fingers brushed something. I pulled it out and stared at the business card Alex had given me when he'd asked me to go to the HOA Christmas party with him.

What day did he say that was? I thought back and then a jolt of surprise shot through me. Tonight. The party was tonight. And Devon would be gone. Was this a sign from the universe that I should go? It was the perfect opportunity to get more information on the HOA board members, and also the perfect opportunity to talk Alex into telling the truth about what he'd heard the night Devon's parents had been killed.

Alex'd overheard one of the suspects, Clyde Lynch, bragging at the bar about the money he was about to come into, less than an hour before he smashed into Devon's parents' boat, killing them both. He'd specifically heard Clyde Lynch say, 'time to earn my money' as he'd left. Unfortunately, someone got to Alex—beat him up pretty badly, left him with a broken jaw—so he'd recanted his testimony, which helped Clyde Lynch get away with murder. I hoped I could change that.

I still had some misgivings about going behind Devon's back. I knew he'd be furious if he found out what I was trying to do. He hated Alex with a passion and had already warned me to stay away from him. But, if I could help Devon bring his parents' killer to justice by doing this, it was worth it. Besides, I wanted to give him something special for Christmas, to let him know how much he means to me. And what would be more special than a way to help convict his parents' murderer? It was decided. I was going.

With a renewed sense of purpose, I began to instruct the class on how to roll up the blankets to create resting poses.

After my second class I pulled my bike out of the storage closet as an experiment. "Come on, Buddha, time for a run."

Sure enough, Buddha pushed himself up slowly and made his way over to me, favoring his back leg. I couldn't believe it. "Buddha!" I started laughing at him, even as I tried to admonish him. "You've been faking it this whole time!"

He plopped down on his haunches and looked up at me with his wide mouth open, tongue hanging out. Then he squinted his eyes and looked away. Yeah, he knew he'd been busted. "All right, you win." I rubbed the top of his head and then put my bike away. "A walk in the gardens it is."

Once my bike was stowed, he happily followed me out of the French doors, without the slightest sign of a limp. I couldn't believe it. "Guess I underestimated you, big guy."

I was standing in the garden, watching Buddha pounce after a lizard, when a text came in from Devon: *Salma says Eva Gold has motive. Bad investments & money troubles. Her brother has been keeping her afloat financially for almost a year. She's also refused to answer any questions.*

Interesting. Eva *could* use the million dollars. So she has motive, not just to smash the statue of Holly, but also to take Ginger.

I texted Devon back: *Does she have an alibi?*

She does not.

Very interesting.

Alex seemed shocked when I called him and told him I'd meet him at the clubhouse for the party. Luckily I still had possession of Hope's black Dior cocktail dress and her promise that she would go to the party, too, to bail me out if Alex got too creepy.

Alex was waiting for me outside the door, his suit jacket slung over one arm.

"Elle!" He beamed at me with a smile that may've once charmed the ladies, but had yellowed with age and lax dental hygiene.

I cringed as he came at me for a hug, and then shoved my hand into his stomach, holding it out for him to shake instead. Hopefully, he'd get the message that just because I'd agreed to accompany him tonight did not give him license to paw at me.

"Good evening, Alex."

Taken aback, his smile faltered as he took my hand. His eyes tracked down my dress. I had a feeling it was muscle memory. "You look amazing tonight."

"Thanks," I answered, forcing myself not to roll my eyes. I suddenly didn't know if I could go through with this. How on earth was I going to convince this man that I was enjoying his company?

"Shall we?" I didn't wait for an answer. Instead I moved through the door and into the clubhouse. I felt his presence behind me like a dark, cologne-saturated shadow.

The clubhouse had been transformed from a meeting hall into a winter wonderland.White lights twinkled over everything and a large buffet had been set up along the back wall, complete with a meat carving station and sushi display. A band was playing Christmas music from a corner stage and couples were already swaying together on the dance floor or standing around chatting at the bar. I scanned the room for Hope and Ira, but I didn't see them yet.

"Let's get a drink," I said, as Alex stood too close to me. If I was going to stomach spending time with him, I'd need some liquid courage.

I downed a shot of whatever their signature Candy Cane drink was tonight and then ordered a glass of wine while Alex got a beer. The warmth traveling to my gut felt like a fire being lit. I could do this.

As we made our way into the center of the room, Alex said, "So, you want to dance? I was known as fancy feet in high school. And not just for my football skills."

I forced a smile. "Maybe later." I needed to get his focus off me. What could distract a guy like him? Then I smiled for real. "So, tell me about your high school football career. You were pretty good, right?"

He grew a little taller. "Good? I was the best."

Jackpot. As he talked about himself, I scanned the room for Eva Gold. I spotted her just as she was pushing through the glass doors that led to the pool area, two men at her heels. One was a dark-haired older gentleman in a tux and the other was younger, but had the same build and dark, wavy hair.

Wait. Was that the Christmas elf who tried to hit on Lulu? Hard to tell from the back but probably, he was Eva's nephew after all. And the older guy could be Eva's brother, Georgy. They even had the same walk.

I had to get out there and see if I was right. *How to ditch Alex for a few minutes?* In desperation, I downed my glass of wine and held it out to him. "Would you be so kind as to get me another glass?"

His expression morphed from surprise to a sly smile as he accepted my empty glass. It wasn't hard to guess what he thought my intoxication would mean. "Whatever you need, I'm at your service."

I fought the grimace that was threatening to manifest, but with the new warmth sprouting in my belly, I managed to keep my voice pleasant. "I'm just going to the ladies' room. I'll meet you back here."

Once I was sure he wouldn't see which direction I was headed, I walked as fast as I dared to the glass doors and slipped outside.

A breeze lifted the cool, damp air from the Gulf and caressed my bare arms. I shivered as my gaze darted around. Spotting the three of them huddled together on the left side of the lighted pool, I removed my heels.

Keeping to the shadows as much as possible, I tiptoed from one palm tree to the next, hopping over the bushes, until I was close enough to hear their conversation. Fortunately it seemed to be rising in volume. I brushed off the mulch sticking to the bottom of my feet and scooted a lizard out of the way as I pressed myself against the base of a Queen Palm.

"I don't know what you mean." Eva's voice was smug and condescending.

"You know very well what I mean, Aunt Eva. Sunny told me what you did and it's not right."

Yep, definitely the Leo Gold kid. What did Eva do? Could he be referring to her smashing the statue and taking Ginger? Would Sunny know about that and not tell the police? Maybe she would hold on to the information in case Eva tried to blackmail her again. If so, that was pretty big information to withhold from the police. Whatever Eva had on her must be bad.

Eva chuckled. "What she did was not right either. And *you* know that."

"That's water under the bridge, Eva," Georgy's voice boomed naturally, like a man used to being in charge.

"Oh, is it?" She sneered. "Ask your son about that."

"It is, Aunt Eva," Leo answered.

"And it's none of your business anyway." Georgy seemed to be losing patience with the conversation. "I'd think you have more important things to worry about."

There was silence and then Eva seemed to deflate. "I did it for you, anyway, Georgy. For all the hard work you put into the Christmas lights display here."

"I know and I appreciate it. Just... be careful. We don't need this kind of scandal."

She had to be talking about smashing Talia's statue.

"And besides, I can take care of my own business," Georgy growled. "No need for you to get involved."

Wait. Take care of his own business? Was Georgy the one who'd smashed the statue? He was definitely the right height. We hadn't even considered him as a suspect.

I held my breath as they walked mere inches from my hiding place. Something crawled across my bare foot. I forced myself to keep still. Their voices faded and then disappeared as they went back inside. I waited a few minutes before jumping out of the mulch with a shiver and slipping back into the party.

SEVENTEEN

My mind was spinning with possibilities and questions... and wine... and I wasn't ready to deal with Alex again. Scanning the crowd, I caught a glimpse of Georgia Waters. Instinctively, I slid behind a potted palm. I had to make sure to stay off that woman's radar tonight.

Then I spotted Leo and his dad, Georgy, on the edge of the dance floor. Leo's hands were shoved in his pockets and his eyes were glued to the floor. Georgy was gesturing wildly about something, his face red. I got closer, waiting for an opportunity to see if he was left-handed. Unfortunately, he trudged away, leaving Leo standing there looking like a scolded puppy.

I approached him. "Leo, right?" I said cheerfully, holding out my hand, proud of myself for being so brave. Or maybe just stupid.

Startled, he glanced up at the sound of his name. It took a moment for him to focus on me, but eventually his softened and he shook my hand. "Yes, I'm sorry. You look familiar but I don't remember catching your name?"

"Elle Pressley and that's perfectly fine. Usually men don't care to catch my name when I'm with Lulu." At his confusion, I added, "Tiny cute girl, amazing green eyes, head full of curls."

His blue eyes sparked with recognition. "Yes, of course, I remember now. I was working on the beach bungalow... in those stupid elf ears," he mumbled. "That's her name then? Your friend who's... expecting?"

"Yes. She really is a sweet girl. She's just been through a horrendous ordeal and has sworn off men at the moment." I remembered her veiled interest in Leo and smiled at the thought of getting her back on the dating horse. I knew from experience that swearing off relationships forever wasn't healthy. I'd done that for years, until I'd met Devon. "If you'd like, I can hold onto your number in case she ever changes her mind. That is, if you don't mind a baby being in the picture." It didn't seem to deter him before but one can never tell.

His smile spread to his eyes. "That would be fantastic." He glanced around and then motioned for me to follow him to the bar. Grabbing a bar napkin, he scribbled down his number. "Look, can you tell her I'm not going to be doing menial labor forever. It's just my dad. He's making me learn the family business from the bottom up. But one day I'll be taking over." He sighed as he handed me the napkin, his voice holding a touch of frustration. "It may take a while."

I smiled, feeling bad for him. "Don't worry. She's not the kind of girl that cares about income bracket."

"Elle, there you are."

We both looked up as Alex approached. He was forcing a smile, while his eyes blinked in confusion at the napkin in my hand. Leaning over, he took in Leo's number. "Hitting on my girl?" His eyes flashed at Leo. "Not cool, bro."

Leo looked amused but said nothing, letting me take the lead.

I simply smiled and tucked the napkin into my sparkly black purse—well, Hope's sparkly black purse—and looked him directly in the eyes. "*Your* girl? You imply ownership where there is none, Alex. *That's* not cool."

Speaking of Hope, where the heck is she? I slipped my glass of wine from Alex's hand and walked off to find her. I didn't know if Alex was following me and, at the moment, I didn't care. He was getting carried away with this whole date thing and needed to be put back in his place.

I found a quiet spot and texted Hope. *Where are you?*

Her reply was immediate. *Almost there. Got stuck in traffic coming back from Tampa. Need rescuing?*

Not yet. Handling it.

K C U soon

I spotted Sunny and Valentino coming off the dance floor. She was wearing an emerald green chiffon dress with a thick silver belt and he was wearing a black tux. Despite their age difference, they did make a nice couple.

Shoot. I should've asked Devon if Valentino gave Salma his DNA willingly. If not, he was still a suspect and so was Sunny. If Valentino was the one who'd smashed Talia's statue, it would've been on her behalf. *Could she be that vindictive of a person?* As I sipped my warm wine and watched Valentino leave her side, I decided to go say hello to Sunny.

"Enjoying the party?" I asked, coming up behind her.

Whirling around, her thin lips formed a polite smile. It didn't reach her eyes. "Yes. The band is excellent this year. You?"

I nodded. "The board throws a lovely party." She was glancing around, seemingly losing interest in small talk, so I decided to try to catch her off guard. "I happened to be at the last board meeting. In the restroom before it started." This got her attention. Her ice-blue eyes cut towards me sharply. "I didn't mean to eavesdrop, but I couldn't help overhearing the conversation... Eva Gold blackmailing you with something she knew. To change your vote about her brother keeping the decorating contract, correct?"

And boom. There it was. The widening of eyes, the flare of nostrils. The almost imperceptible mixture of anger, guilt and surprise. Then her face relaxed as she regained control of her emotions. I watched her take in a deep, slow breath in through her nose. Then she nodded in concession.

Touching my arm gently with a slender hand, she leaned in with a ghost of a smile. "You're young, Dear, unversed in the ways of how calculating women can be. My advice, never share a secret with a friend because you never know when that friend will become your enemy."

"So, you consider Eva Gold your enemy?"

Dog Gone | 171

A perfectly plucked and penciled-in brow raised in amusement. "Well, I certainly don't consider her my friend."

I nodded. I needed more. Time to push her a bit. "Speaking of secrets. I'll let you in on one." I moved closer to her and put on my most earnest expression. "The night Talia Hill's dog nanny, Diggs, was murdered, the police think whoever did it was there to destroy the glass statue of her dog, Holly. The one the HOA board wanted her to remove. Even if the board member didn't swing the hammer, but had someone else do it, they would be guilty of accessory to murder." I wasn't sure if that was true or not, I was just looking to shake her tree a bit and see what fell out.

"Oh?"

I watched her for any signs of panic or guilt. Her face was smooth, unreadable. In fact, she seemed bored and then her eyes glittered happily. I turned to see where her attention had gone. Of course, Valentino was back.

Handing her a glass of wine he nodded at me, his eyes narrowing. "Miss Pressley, wasn't it?"

I felt a prickle of discomfort at his dark, intense gaze. It didn't look friendly at all. "Yes. Hello, good to see you again."

Shoving a hand in his black slack's pocket, he glanced around. "Haven't seen your P.I. boyfriend around tonight. I wanted to thank him for sending the police to swab my cheek."

Ouch. He was definitely angry. Why did he think Devon was the one who sent the police? Salma would never throw Devon under the bus like that. Guess he just put two and two together since we'd been there questioning him. Might as well go all in. "And did you give them one?"

He didn't blink. "Of course. I have nothing to hide."

I nodded and glanced at Sunny. "It wasn't just you they wanted to swab, Valentino. Would it surprise either of you to know Eva Gold wouldn't cooperate with the police?"

Valentino cocked his head and glanced at Sunny. She was shaking her head. "Not in the least. That woman wouldn't cooperate with God if He was standing right in front of her." Then Sunny's demeanor softened as she changed the subject. "Elle, you teach that quaint little doga class at the Pampered Pup Spa, right?" When I nodded, her eyes lit up. "Do you happen to do private classes? My Leona just doesn't get along with other dogs, so I haven't been able to attend. Heard great things from the ladies, though."

"Sure." I dug a business card out of Hope's purse. "Give me a call. We can set something up." Hopefully soon. I would either have a solid suspect or a new client.

They both looked behind me. My body tensed. I knew who would be standing there when I turned around. Time to deal with the second reason I came here tonight.

"Excuse me," I said to Sunny and Valentino. Turning to face Alex, I was surprised to see Hope standing there grinning at me instead. In relief, I wrapped my arms around her. "Thank heavens," I whispered, as she squeezed me back.

She grabbed my hand. "Come and refresh your drink with me and tell me what's been going on so far."

We moved through the crowd, which was getting merrier by the minute, to the bar. "Oh that food smells divine. I'm starving," she said, getting in line. "We haven't had time to eat since breakfast."

"Where's Ira?" I asked, looking around.

"He got caught by one of his golfing buddies outside." She made a twirling motion with her hand. "Sooo... what's going on? Have you talked to Alex yet?"

I shook my head. "I've been busy learning more about Eva Gold and Sunny."

She gave me a chastising but sympathetic look. "Remember why you put yourself in this God-awful situation to begin with. For Devon."

"I know." I groaned. "I'm working up to it." I raised my half-empty wine glass as evidence then glanced around. "I hope I haven't run him off. I haven't been the most polite date." *Understatement of the year.*

We stepped up to the bar. Hope ordered two shots of tequila and two glasses of wine. Clinking our shot glasses, her face serious, she said, "To doing what's necessary for justice."

"Amen," I whispered. We both grimaced after downing the shot and grabbed our wineglasses. I consolidated mine, hoping it would be enough to get me through what I was about to do next. "Ok, I'm going in. If he hasn't ditched me. Wish me luck."

She gave my hand one more squeeze. "Luck. You can do this. For Devon."

I checked the hallway where the restrooms were first, wondering if he was waiting for me there. Instead I found Georgia Waters. She practically ran into me on her way out of the ladies' room.

"Well, well, well." She sneered, looking me up and down. "If it isn't little Miss Cinderella all dressed up in someone else's clothes. Come for the free food?"

Her words were like a vice around my chest. The humiliation set my face on fire, but I'd had enough to drink that, instead of freezing or having an anxiety attack, I opened my mouth and unleashed my own attack.

"I'm sorry, Georgia. I'm sorry you're so miserable that you have to spend all your energy trying to make other people miserable, too. And I'm sorry you're so insecure about your relationship with Sammy you had to stoop to tipping off the press about where the ransom exchange would be. Yeah, we know it was you. What a petty, petty thing to do. But, I would expect nothing less from you." My body was shaking but I didn't care. Her mouth had dropped and she had nothing to say for once, so I added, "Not that you don't have a right to be jealous. I was there when Sammy came to Talia's house, and I could see the love he still has for her in his eyes. Who can blame him, though. She's so sweet and kind. Just such an easy person to love. God knows why he'd leave her for a mean-spirited, gold-digger like you."

Her face drained of color. Her blue eyes had narrowed and were glittering dangerously. Time to go. Whirling around on my heels—and catching myself on the wall before I fell over—I hurried away without a glance back. I half-expected to feel a yank on my hair, or her jumping on my back, but I made it to the dance floor without being attacked.

I was already regretting that little speech. It didn't feel good to say those things to her, even though they were true. Resting a hand on my stomach to settle it down, I took a few steadying breaths and continued my search for Alex. I finally found him sulking over a big plate of roast beef. Stopping to gather my courage, I pushed myself forward.

"Hey, there you are," I said, keeping Devon in the forefront of my mind as a reminder of why I was torturing myself tonight. "I'm ready for that dance now."

Alex looked up from his plate, his expression one of suspicion. "Really?"

I nodded with a tight smile. It was the best I could do.

"All right." Still keeping a wary eye on me, Alex found a place to set his plate down and then stood there awkwardly.

"All right." I repeated, setting down my glass. "Let's do this."

The dance floor was crowded and high volume, with people laughing and trying to talk over each other. I led him to the edge by the front door, hoping it was far enough from the band to be able to hear each other or this was going to be for nothing. He seemed to be less skeptical as I let him slide his hands to my lower back. As I lifted my hands to rest on his shoulders, I kept my arms stiff so he couldn't pull me into him. His cologne could've knocked out a horse. His palms were hot and damp through the cocktail dress. I forced myself to relax and focus.

He leaned toward my face. "Have I told you that you look beautiful tonight, as always."

I dropped my head, trying to escape the smell of roast beef and cologne. Not a pleasant combination.

Come on, Elle. You can do this. Use your womanly wiles, whatever that means.

Raising my chin, I said, "Thank you. And thanks for inviting me. This is a great party. Very festive." How was I going to bring up the night Devon's parents were killed and what he knew? "I haven't been much in the Christmas spirit this year."

"Why not?" Alex asked, his hands sliding down to rest on my hips.

I unclenched my teeth so I could answer him. "Well, you know... Devon's been in an awful mood ever since Clyde Lynch was released from prison. I mean, how would you feel if you knew someone had gotten away with murdering your parents?"

"Terrible, of course. I'm not an animal." His chin jerked back and his gaze slipped off mine. When he looked back down at me, his suspicion had returned. "So, you and Devon are still... together?"

We wouldn't be if he knew I was here. "For the moment, yes." True enough. Here goes nothing. I held his gaze. "Alex, it's very flattering that you... like me. I know there's a good guy in here." I rested a palm on his chest. "A guy who would do the right thing, even if it's the hard thing. Even if it's the dangerous thing. Because, you're not a coward. Are you?"

His face twisted with offense. "Of course not."

"I thought not," I said gently. "So, think for a moment if it were your parents who were killed... murdered. And someone knew something that could put the people involved behind bars for a long time. But that someone wouldn't come forward with the information because they'd been threatened. Well, wouldn't you think that person was a coward? Do you really want Devon Burke thinking you're a coward?"

He stopped moving but his hands squeezed my hips firmly. "Look, Elle..." His gaze suddenly moved behind me and a dark cloud passed over his face. "Speak of the devil."

EIGHTEEN

I closed my eyes. *Oh God, please no.* I didn't want to look, but I had to know. Dropping my hands, I turned slowly and our eyes met.

Devon stood there in the doorway, his expression and his body completely still. But his eyes said it all. They were a hot, blue fire filled with disbelief, pain and anger. Time seemed frozen and all the noise of the party fell away. There was only the sound of my heart and blood pounding in my ears. All I could do was wait. Wait for him to turn and walk out of my life forever.

But instead, he slowly buttoned his suit jacket and moved toward us with the grace of a panther stalking its prey, his eyes and anger fixed on Alex. I stepped in front of him at the last second, seeing the murderous intention in his eyes.

"Devon, don't," I whispered through a constricted throat and heart. "It's not worth it."

His gaze swung to me and almost knocked me back. I'd never had his anger directed at me before and it stung like a slap. Tears pricked my eyes. I tried to apologize but I was frozen, like a gazelle staring into the face of the lion. Only I wasn't afraid *of* him, I was afraid *for* him. "Please," I managed.

His gaze tracked down to my hip where Alex still had one hand resting, then back up to Alex behind me. His neck was flushed. His jaw twitched. His whole body tensed and exuded a threat. "Kindly get your bloody hand off of my girlfriend." His voice was a whisper but held the threat of violence as surely as if he'd yelled.

I felt the warmth leave my hip. Maybe Alex wasn't so dumb after all.

Then Devon slipped his hand in mine. "Let's go."

We'd only made it a handful of steps before Alex yelled, "Hey, Elle can make her own choice. She's a grown woman."

Or he *is* as dumb as I thought.

Devon stopped abruptly, his hand squeezing mine, his other hand curling into a fist. I could feel his body vibrating. I wrapped my hand firmly around Devon's arm and turned back to Alex. "It's okay. I'll be fine."

Devon continued forward, pulling me through the doors into the outside air.

"Elle! Devon! Wait!" Hope was running behind to catch up with us.

I stopped in my tracks, pulling him up short, needing the presence of my best friend, my rock, at this moment. "Devon, wait."

Reluctantly he stopped, then dropped my hand and began pacing, running his hands through his hair feverishly.

It was hard to watch, knowing I did this to him. I hurt him this bad and there was nothing I could say to fix it. The image of me in Alex's arms would be burned into his memory. The tears fell. I'd never felt so helpless. *What have I done?*

Hope reached me, wrapped her arms around me. "It"ll be okay," she whispered in my ear. "He loves you." Then turning to Devon she yelled, "Stop acting like the jealous boyfriend for one minute and listen."

Her raised voice worked. Devon stopped in his tracks and turned an exasperated stare on her.

Hope glared right back. "She did this for you, you know. Put herself in the crosshairs of a man she can't stand to try and change his mind about testifying against the dirtbags who murdered *your* parents."

He moved closer to us, his hands perched on his hips, his eyes darting between us and then finally resting on me. "You lied to me, Elle. Purposefully. You didn't tell me you were coming here tonight. With…" he threw a hand back at the building. "With him. It was a betrayal of trust."

I wanted to run into his arms. To just hold him. I knew that's what we both needed right now, but I couldn't handle the rejection if he pushed me away. It would crush me. So, instead I held my ground and tried to reach him with my eyes, pleading for him to understand. "And what would you have said if I'd told you my plan to come here and try to talk some sense into Alex?"

"Not to go, of course." His Irish accent grew thicker with his anger.

"Exactly. But I had to try."

"It's not worth it, Elle." Devon's anger dissolved into pain.

Hope's arms were crossed tightly as she watched our exchange. "It's not worth Elle spending a few hours with Alex to have a chance at putting your parents' murderers behind bars? You know that's not true."

Devon shook his head. "He"ll never testify."

Hope argued back. "But what if he will? What if he just needed someone to call him out as the coward he is?"

Devon rubbed his forehead. "I just... I just... can't right now." He lifted his head. "Elle, will ya come home with me now?"

The sadness in his voice hit me like a gut punch. With a mixture of relief that he even still wanted me at his house and dread at what the night held, I hugged Hope, promising to call her tomorrow and followed Devon to his Jeep. I'd pick up my car tomorrow. There was no way I was leaving his side tonight.

A silence filled the space between us on the drive home. A silence that wasn't empty at all, but pregnant with unspoken words, unwieldy emotions. Hurt. Sadness. Fear. Anger. Love. A storm was raging between us, and it seemed neither of us trusted ourselves to open our mouth for fear of what would come out. I swallowed the panic that threatened to blossom into a full-fledged attack.

Instead we moved like broken robots. The Christmas lights and wiry snowman seemed to mock our sadness as we entered the house and greeted the dogs. Buddha's warm body was a welcomed comfort as I buried my face in his fur, and he licked the tear away that had broken free.

Devon held the door open wider. "I'll take them down for a spell on the beach."

Nodding, I went and checked on my mother. Luckily, she was snoring peacefully. My body collapsed against the door frame, and I stayed there for God knows how long, watching her with a deepening sadness. How do you force someone to care about themselves? To value themselves? Did my biological father have a hand in destroying her self-worth when he left her pregnant with me? Or had she always been this way? I'd never know. Her childhood was one of a hundred things she'd never speak of.

The nurse's soft footsteps padded behind me from the bedroom across the hall. "I got her to walk around the yard today, but she's still refusing to eat anything except peanut butter and jelly."

"That's all she thinks she deserves," I whispered.

"What's that?" she asked.

I sighed. "Nevermind. I'll talk to her tomorrow." I pushed my drained body off the wall. "You're a life saver. Thanks for being here for her."

I took a moment to gather my courage before I entered the bedroom, expecting Devon to be sitting on the edge of the bed, waiting to start the argument that was inevitable. Surprisingly, the room was empty. Buddha trotted in from the opened front door and gently nudged my hand. He'd brought in the scent of seawater with him. Devon must still be down on the beach with Petey.

"I'm all right, big guy. Mommy just did something really dumb." I scratched his ears and kissed the spot between his eyes. "Go lay down." Instead, he followed me around as I slipped out of the cocktail dress, shoes and jewelry. I desperately needed to wash Alex's cologne off my body. Under the cover of the shower noise and steam, I released the tears that I'd managed to mostly hold in check.

When I was scrubbed raw, my skin red, my emotions emptied, I opened the bathroom door and peered out. The room was dark. The two dogs were stretched out on the bed. Devon was nowhere to be found.

Quickly drying off and slipping into an oversized t-shirt, I flipped on the light. There, on my nightstand, was a note. My heart dropped like a stone. With shaking hands I opened it and read:

"Elle, I need some time to sort through things, spending the night inland. We'll talk tomorrow. Devon"

Clutching the note to my heart, I fell back on the bed. I stared up at the ceiling fan, wishing I could go back in time and change this night. Forget about my stupid plan with Alex. Devon was right. He wouldn't ever testify anyway. All I'd managed to do was hurt the one man I would die for.

Will he ever be able to forgive me? What if it was he who had betrayed me, with my worst enemy? What if he went off behind my back with Georgia Waters? Would it matter if it was for a good reason? Closing my eyes, the tears ran down into my ears. No, if I found him in her arms it wouldn't matter at all. I'd never be able to erase that image from my memory.

I cuddled up with the dogs. Then my eyes popped opened.

Wait, how did Devon know I was at the Christmas party anyway? Of course. Georgia Waters. She must've called him. I should've known she'd get even. Why couldn't that woman just mind her own business? How many relationships did she intend on wrecking in one lifetime. Was there some homewrecker award she was going for?

"Ug," I growled, pressing my face into Buddha's white fur to keep from screaming.

There was no way I was going to be able to sleep tonight. I got up, threw on a pair of yoga pants and a jacket over the long t-shirt. I had to do something to keep my mind off of Devon.

I thought about Georgy as a possible suspect. Not being a Moon Key resident, he had to have come here tonight either via the ferry or his own boat. Most likely, his own boat. Would he be arrogant enough to drive it here if he was the dognapper? Only one way to find out. I'd have to check the guest marina. Luckily the Christmas party would go on late into the night.

It took me thirty minutes to walk down Moon Key Drive, past the private marina and waterfront condos. The fresh air cleared my mind and I remembered what the boat was called. It was a Bowrider. When I finally arrived at the guest marina I pulled up an image of a Bowrider on my phone so I knew what I was looking for. It'd been too dark, and too much going on, the night of the botched ransom attempt for me to know the boat by sight.

I strode down the sidewalk beneath a row of tall, skinny palm trees. Boats were tied up on both sides of the marina and along the wooden walkway in the middle. Lots of boats. Visibility was limited, with just a single lamp glowing yellow in each corner of the marina and heavy cloud cover. I'd have to start from one end and make my way around.

As I walked to the far left corner, a boat engine roared to life. I whirled around. I couldn't see past the sailboats and mini-yachts tied up in front of me, so I took off down the wooden deck.

Tripping on an uneven board, I stumbled forward and fell on my hands and knees. My palms stung. Ignoring the pain, I pushed myself up and ran. I hit the corner and made a right, sucking air hard. By the time I got to the end of the dock, the boat had made the turn behind the seawall and was almost out of the no-wake zone. With one more burst of energy, I climbed up onto the stone seawall and caught my first glimpse of the boat. It's dark, wedged shape could definitely be a Bowrider. Two dark figures stood in the hull. Was that Georgy? And maybe his son with him? No way to tell. The boat took off, cutting through the water, leaving a white wedge of wake behind.

Resting my hands on my knees, I leaned over to catch my breath.

I spent another forty-five minutes walking the marina just to be sure, but there were no other blue and white Bowriders there. Luck was not on my side tonight.

NINETEEN

Tuesday morning found me exhausted from restless bouts of sleep and checking my phone constantly for any word from Devon. I decided to skip my yoga practice on the beach before work. Just getting dressed was taking more energy than I had. I watched the dogs play in the backyard for a few minutes and then realized something. With all the drama yesterday, I hadn't heard any news from Talia. The dognapper had got his ransom money Sunday night. Surely, if he was planning on returning Ginger, he would've found time to do it yesterday. No news was not good news.

I hurried back in, grabbed my phone and called Talia. No answer. I left a message and then texted her. *Please call me!*

I heard the nurse moving about, so I went to the kitchen and made Mom an almond butter and spinach smoothie. When I walked in, the nurse was taking her blood pressure.

"Morning," the nurse offered.

Mom glared at me. "Well, look who decided to grace our presence. And no, it's not a good morning. I didn't get any sleep because of all that racket those dogs made at two o'clock in the morning."

I frowned. The dogs had barked at the door in the middle of the night but they'd calmed down and came back to bed fairly quickly. "Sorry, Mom. I'll close them in the bedroom tonight."

She apparently was in the mood to pick a fight because she added, "And when are you gonna do something with that rat's nest hair of yours?"

I ignored her attempt to hurt me or suck me into an argument. Either way, I had neither the energy nor patience to deal with her today. "Mom, you're going to have to get some nutrition in you. I've accommodated your sweet tooth as much as possible, but you have to meet me half-way. You will drink this." I put it on the nightstand and walked out.

She was saying something to the nurse about the way I treat her, but my thoughts were on Talia. Still no text or call back. The sick feeling in my stomach grew.

When I opened the front door to leave, something white fluttered to the ground. I picked it up. It was a piece of folded typing paper. Buddha pushed past me as I unfolded it and read the typed words:

STOP INTERFERING OR THE DOG DIES

Adrenaline shot through my body as I glanced around the yard. This must've been what the dogs were barking about last night. My anxiety ticked up several notches. The killer had been standing on our front porch in the middle of the night. I glanced behind me for any sign of Angel. When I didn't see her, I felt a little better.

Heading back to the kitchen, I found a plastic baggie and dropped in the note. I locked the door behind me, checking it twice before I found Buddha sitting in the empty driveway. *Crap.* I forgot I'd left my car at the clubhouse last night. And my bike was in the closet at the studio.

"Guess we're walking."

A few minutes into our walk down Moon Key Drive, a black sedan pulled up beside us.

"Elle?" a familiar voice called.

Waving, I led Buddha over to the car. "Good morning, Salma." I nodded at the driver. "Officer." Adjusting the yoga mat bag on my shoulder, I asked, "What're you two doing on Moon Key this morning?"

Salma removed her sunglasses. "Devon found out Eva Gold gave her maid paid vacation for Christmas, which is uncharacteristic and unlikely considering her money troubles. We're going back to interview her again. Didn't trust that she'd make it to the station. You need a ride somewhere?"

I felt a tiny stab to my heart. Devon didn't tell me that. Of course, when would he have? After he found me in his enemy's arms? "Sure. That'd be great. We're heading to the Pampered Pup."

"Hop in."

I crinkled my nose at the smell of disinfectant in the backseat. "So, Eva. She's your number one suspect?"

Salma glanced back at me. "She's a strong suspect." Then she sighed. "I shouldn't be discussing this with you, but I suppose Devon will tell you anyway. Sunny's friend, Valentino, his DNA didn't match what we got off the collar. I'm reluctant to rule him out though." She reached down at her feet and then handed me a sheet of paper. "Take a look at that and tell me who you think it looks like."

I studied the computer-generated photo of a man's face. "This was created from Sammy's description of the guy on the boat?"

"Yep," she said, her arm stretched back to give Buddha a scratch under the chin.

"The dark wavy hair, the high cheek bones. It does look like Valentino."

"That's what we think, too." She took the paper back. "But Sammy's not sure he got a good enough look for this to be accurate. He only had a few seconds struggle with the guy in the dark before he was knocked out of the boat. We'll still keep an eye on him anyway. By the way, Devon said Talia completed the ransom drop Sunday night. Any word on whether he's returned her dog?"

I shook my head. "He got his money but no, I haven't heard any news from Talia yet."

"A shame." We pulled around the fountain and stopped in front of the Pampered Pup. "Well, if we get anything suspicious from Eva Gold, we'll be able to get a search warrant for her property. Maybe we'll get lucky and a search will turn up Ginger there."

I didn't say what I was thinking... turn her up alive was the question. I dug into my yoga bag and pulled out the baggie with the threatening note. "I found this on my front door this morning. It's a threat to stop investigating. The dogs were barking around two this morning so, I think that's when it was left."

Salma pulled on a glove and opened the note. Her face darkened. "All right, I'll get this analyzed, though I doubt the person touched it with bare hands. They haven't been that reckless so far. And tell Devon he really needs to get security cameras up around that place."

I nodded. "Will do. Thanks for the ride."

Dragging myself and Buddha through the Christmas music and decorations in the lobby, and managing a few forced smiles, I made it to my doga studio and closed the French doors firmly behind me. Leaning against them, I fought the well of tears once again. If I was going to be fighting my emotions all day, it was going to be a very long day.

I took in a deep breath. Blew it out. Repeated until I didn't feel on the verge of losing my mind.

The sketch Salma had shown me came floating back. I'd immediately thought of Valentino because that's who we'd just been discussing but... now that I thought about it, it also looked a bit like Georgy.

A low, friendly *woof!* came from Buddha at my feet. I opened my eyes. There, sitting in the middle of my studio, was the spirit form of my childhood dog, Angel.

Crap. Angel's visits never failed to precede danger.

I thanked my little ghostly guardian and promised her I'd be careful. She stayed for a few seconds and lifted her paw before fading. I choked back the hot tears that familiar gesture brought on. *Good heavens, Elle, you're a mess.* Now, besides being heartbroken over the situation with Devon, frustrated with my mother and worried about Talia, I also had to watch my back.

As I put on some calming music, I noticed my hands trembling. I'd have to bury myself in work. It was all I could do.

As the ladies and their dogs began to file in, I forced a cheery greeting. There was no fooling Beth Anne and

Violet, though. They unrolled their mats and then approached me with their arms crossed.

"What's happened?" Beth Anne asked, as Shakespeare greeted Buddha with lots of sniffing and tail wagging.

"Nothing, why?" I squeaked out. Even Buddha looked up at me with an unconvinced stare. My posture deflated. "Everything." I told them about what I'd done to Devon and about not being able to reach Talia, fearing the worst for Ginger, and about the threatening note I'd found on my doorstep this morning.

"Oh, Elle." Violet gave me a tight hug, her spiky red hair prickling my cheek. "First of all, you have a lot to learn about men. You hurt Devon's ego, that's all. He's a good guy, though, and he's crazy about you. He'll come around." Beth Anne was nodding in agreement. "And as far as the threatening note is concerned, that just means you and Devon are on the right track. He won't let anything happen to you." She paused and then shared a glance with Beth Anne. "Now Talia not calling yet, that is troubling, but let's not worry until we know something for sure." She clapped her hands. "But, in the positive news department, Beth Anne found out what Eva Gold could be using to blackmail Sunny with. Tell her."

Beth Anne glanced behind her and then leaned in closer to us. "So, I found out from Celia Barns, who dated Georgy Gold for a while, that one of Sunny's previous boyfriends was apparently underage."

I stared at her. "Underage? Like under the age of twenty-one?"

"Like under the age of eighteen." Her eyebrows rose.

Violet smirked.

I shook my head slowly, as if that would help process this information. "Besides being really creepy, she could go to jail for that, right?"

"Yep. Hence the term *jail bait*," Violet said.

I thought about what this new piece of information meant, but I couldn't fit it into the puzzle. "Well, it's scandalous but I don't think it has anything to do with Talia and Ginger. What we really need is to find out who wanted that statue gone bad enough to destroy it themselves. And commit murder to cover it up."

"And steal Ginger for a million dollar ransom," Beth Anne added.

I rubbed my forehead. "I feel like we're out of time. At least Ginger is." A hopelessness settled over me that was heavier than any emotion I'd ever felt. I plopped down on my mat. "Thanks," I said, mumbling something about starting class.

Beth Anne leaned down in front of me. "Are you sure you're all right to teach today?"

I nodded, feeling numb. "I need to keep busy."

"Tell you what," Violet said, resting a hand on my shoulder. "If you haven't heard from Talia by the time your next class is over, we'll go pay her a visit."

"Good idea." I nodded, feeling a little better.

Beth Anne, Violet and I all piled into Beth Anne's Ford Expedition with our dogs. I still hadn't been able to reach Talia on the phone and was getting more worried by the second. When we arrived at her place the gates were closed and locked for the first time. I pushed the call button and a familiar voice answered.

"Marcel, it's Elle. Is Talia all right? I haven't been able to reach her. Can we come in?"

"I'm sorry, Miss Elle. She's... fine but she doesn't want to see anyone right now."

I peered through the gate, biting my lip. This was not good. I mashed the button again. "Marcel, she shouldn't be alone right now. Please, let us see her."

"I wish I could." His voice broke and then lowered. "She's in quite a depressed state. She won't eat or sleep. But I'm sorry, I have to obey her wishes."

My forehead hit the call box. "I understand. Will you try to talk to her? Tell her I really need to see her."

"I'll try, Miss Elle."

"Thanks, Marcel."

With one final helpless glance through the gate, I made my way back to the black SUV and climbed in. It smelled like pine and dog breath. "She won't see anybody. Marcel said she's not eating or sleeping. We have to find some way to talk to her."

"We could scale the gate," Violet said, eyeing it like she was considering it.

"Then what?" Beth Anne asked. "Break a window?"

"I appreciate your enthusiasm but we can't force her to talk to us. We can only be there when she's ready." I checked my phone again. No messages or calls. She wasn't the only one I couldn't force to talk to me. *Devon, where are you?* "Let's go."

After my four o'clock class, I closed and locked the studio doors and turned to face the holiday cheer in the lobby. In front of the towering Christmas tree now sat an oversized gold chair with a man in a Santa suit. He was holding two white Chihuahuas in his lap—one wearing a green sweater, one in red. I wondered if it was the same Santa that Devon had made friends with at the party. The dog in the red sweater kept jumping up trying to pull at his beard. The other one looked like it was going to flee at the first opportunity. When the camera flash went off, that's exactly what it did.

"Pip! Come here!" squealed his owner.

There was a cluster of dogs and owners waiting their turn in a line around the lobby. I hoped Rita was paying Santa well.

I'd called Hope to pick me and Buddha up and take me to my car. Better to wait for her outside where I'd only have to face some lights and a few mechanical flamingos with Santa hats. And make small talk with the guard. "Hey, Marvin. How's things?"

He reached down and scratched Buddha's head with a large hand. "Evening, Elle. Quiet here. Just enjoying the cooler weather. Yourself?" Buddha was nudging his pocket. He chuckled.

"Not a big fan of the cooler weather but I don't have to work outdoors. And go ahead, he can have one. Just make him sit first."

Buddha inhaled the treat and licked his lips, looking hopefully up at Marvin, who chuckled and checked his hand playfully. "Thanks for leaving my fingers in place."

Hope's black Jaguar pulled smoothly around the fountain.

"Have a good night."

"Thanks," I said, sinking into the soft leather seat of Hope's car. "You're a lifesaver."

As we navigated the crowded street toward the clubhouse and my abandoned car, she kept throwing worried glances my way.

"I'm fine," I assured her.

"Liar," she said. "Talk."

"Has anyone ever told you you're bossy?" Folding my arms, I spoke to her glove box. "I haven't heard from Devon yet today. He's probably finding a crappy rental apartment to move me into to get me out of his life."

Hope snorted. "You and your imagination."

"And Talia is holed up in her mansion, not eating or sleeping or seeing anyone."

"Losing a pet is hard. She'll be okay... eventually."

I glanced up at her. I guess I hadn't accepted yet that it was over, that Ginger was gone, because her words struck me hard. "Do you really think she'll never see Ginger again?"

Hope's brown eyes softened as she nodded. "I'm sorry."

A sick feeling in my stomach pushed aside the numbness as we pulled up to my Beetle.

Hope reached over and hugged me. "Hey, don't worry. Devon just needs some time. You guys will work it out."

"I don't know, Hope. I really screwed up. But, I'm actually more worried about Talia right now. I don't know her well enough to know if she'd... you know, harm herself. She seems so fragile. And she's already lost Holly. I just wish she would talk to me."

Hope nodded. "I wish she would, too. Just keep trying. Maybe one of these times, she'll pick up."

"You're right. It's all I can do, I guess." I opened the door and let Buddha out of the back seat.

"Let me know as soon as you hear from either of them," Hope said.

"I will. Goodnight."

The musty smell of the sun-cracked seats was more pronounced having just come from the leather and lemony smell of Hope's new Jaguar. I cranked the engine and my car sputtered to life. "Well, at least I have you, Buddha. What more does a girl need." I reached over and scratched under his chin, getting a string of slobber on my forearm. Somehow it was comforting.

As I was about to back out of the parking space, my phone buzzed. My heart leapt. *Devon?* Shoving the gearshift back into park, I grabbed my phone.

The message was from Devon, but it wasn't at all what I'd expected.

Something's happened. Meet at the guest marina asap

TWENTY

I stared at Buddha, a million questions running through my mind. *Devon's on Moon Key? When did he get back?* "What do you think's happened, boy?" Buddha cocked his head. "You're right, only one way to find out." With a trembling hand, I fought the gearshift, wincing as it made a loud scraping sound and then, finally, wrangled it into reverse.

I was only three minutes away. As we rumbled noisily down the narrow, palm tree lined road that led to the marina parking lot, I could already see the activity. Car lights crisscrossed the mostly empty lot, while a red ambulance light pulsed in the trees. As soon as I pulled in, I was ordered to stop by a young uniformed officer. He approached my window as I rolled it down.

"Evening, Officer—" I began. Buddha started barking frantically, his paws on the dashboard, slinging saliva onto the window. "Buddha!" I yelled. He didn't stop. Confused and terrified as I saw the officer back up a step and place his hand on his gun, I grabbed his collar. "Buddha! Enough!"

Buddha finally glanced at me and then rested his haunches back on the seat, his intense stare focused somewhere in front of us, a pathetic whine building in his barrel chest. "I'm sorry, Officer, he's not dangerous. Something's just got him worked up."

A figure approached us. "It's all right. She's with me."

Devon! Thank heavens.

The officer nodded and pointed to the dark, empty corner of the lot. "Just leave your vehicle over there, ma'am."

"I'll wait for you over there," Devon said, pointing to the circle of black sedans, police cars and a firetruck. Then glancing in the window, he frowned at Buddha. "Better leave him in the car for now."

"You be a good boy," I said breathlessly, kissing Buddha on the head. "Stay." I rolled the windows down halfway, even though the night was in the low 60's, and rushed over to Devon.

He was standing with Salma. Both of them had their arms crossed as I approached.

"What's happened?" I managed. Breathing was starting to get difficult as my chest tightened with anxiety.

"Hi, Elle." She glanced at Devon. "Go on, fill her in. I'm going to check on the progress."

Devon reached out and touched my fingers, bringing them gently into the fold of his hand, then he smiled. "There's good news and bad news."

"Good news first please."

As he opened his mouth, a faint bark echoed through the night air. A responding bark came from Buddha. My head whipped around to the circle of cars. "Oh God, please tell me that's Ginger," I whispered.

"That's Ginger," Devon said. I could hear the relief in his voice. And I could see it in his face as I looked back up at him.

"She's all right?" I couldn't believe it.

"She is, as far as we can tell."

I leaped forward and wrapped my arms around his neck with a cry. "She is!"

When I pulled back, I felt his hands stay on my waist, holding me there. Then he seemed to catch himself and released me. I decided not to think about that at the moment. "Does Talia know yet?"

"We couldn't reach her. Salma's sent a car to her home. Hopefully she'll know soon."

I couldn't stop smiling. After all the stress and worry, it didn't seem possible it was over. Ginger was going home. "So, what's the bad news?"

He pointed at the bulk of the activity. "The apparent dognapper is dead."

I stared at all the vehicles, the flashing lights. "Was there a shoot-out? Who is it?"

"There was no shoot-out. He was found in the truck, already deceased. Ginger was in a crate beside him. Salma thinks he may've been trying to make a run for it by boat tonight and had a heart attack or somethin'. Though, they haven't found a blue and white Bowrider in the marina. A suitcase full of money was in the back of the truck, so Talia'll get whatever's left of the million returned along with Ginger. There was also a toolbox with a hammer that they'll test for Diggs's DNA." Devon turned to watch the bursts of flash as the forensic photographer worked. "The ME will be able to tell more about the young fella's death upon examination."

I shook my head in disbelief. The dognapper keeling over from a heart attack moments before he escaped Moon Key with Ginger? Especially a young man? That seemed a little too tidy to me. "Was there ID in the truck?"

"There was. His name was Leo Gold."

Shock silenced me. I pictured Leo's handsome face as I spoke to him at the HOA Christmas party. I remembered him writing down his number for me to give to Lulu. He did write with his left hand. And he was the right height. Then I thought about the police sketch Salma had shown me. Of course, I can see the likeness to him, now that I know.

Devon kept talking. "Probably related to the Gold family somehow, which doesn't look very good for Eva. Salma's thinkin' Eva must've hired Leo Gold to destroy the statue. When Diggs surprised him, he knocked him on the head and decided to take Ginger for ransom."

"Huh," was all I could manage. Leo Gold being the killer hadn't even crossed my mind. He seemed so nice. Heavens, I'd almost set Lulu up with a murderer. At that thought, I felt faint. "He was Eva's nephew, true. But I don't get why he'd risking taking Ginger for ransom? His family has plenty of money."

Devon shrugged. "Young lads do stupid, irrational things."

I wrapped my arms around my body, unable to get Leo's smile out of my mind. I couldn't believe he was dead. He was so young and had such a bright future ahead of him running his father's company. *Didn't he?*

Then I remembered something he'd said and turned to Devon. "You know, his father was making him learn the family business from the ground up, so maybe he didn't have access to the family money. The first time I met him, he was putting up Christmas lights outside the bungalow, wearing elf ears. Maybe it was too humiliating for him, and he wanted to get out from under his father's thumb. Georgy Gold doesn't seem like the nicest of fathers. And I've been thinking about Georgy being a possible suspect. Maybe it wasn't Eva, but Georgy who put Leo up to smashing the statue. Even though he doesn't live on Moon Key, Georgy could've been offended by Talia's statue of Holly."

"Anything's possible at this point. Where did you meet Georgy Gold?" Devon asked.

Before I had to answer that, and bring up the HOA Christmas party, I caught a glimpse of white fur running between two patrol cars. "Oh no! Buddha!" I took off after him, my legs shaking like Jell-O. *They wouldn't shoot him, would they?* Devon's feet pounded behind me.

We reached the circle of people just in time to hear, "Whoa! Where'd that dog come from?"

"No!" I shrieked, pushing my way past a few officers. "He's mine. I got him."

"It's all right," I heard Salma yell. "He's friendly."

I collapsed onto Buddha, grabbing his collar and gulping air. I didn't have the breath left to scold him, though I really wanted to. Especially because he was looking so pleased with himself. I glanced from his moon-eyed stare to the object of his affection.

Ginger lay in the wire crate, her head resting on her paws. Her eyebrows ticked up as her round, black eyes moved from Buddha to me. No wagging tail.

My heart squeezed. I scratched her paw with one finger through the wire. "Oh, Ginger. It's all right girl. You'll be back with your mom soon."

"They're on their way with Talia now," Salma said from above me.

I released Buddha's collar and stood. "This news couldn't have come soon enough. Talia was so depressed."

"At least it'll be a happy ending for someone." Salma shook her head as she glanced into the cab of the rusty truck beside us.

I followed her gaze and my stomach clenched, roiled and threatened to push up my dinner. My hand went to my mouth.

Leo had fallen forward, and his head rested on the steering wheel. Luckily I couldn't see his face, but a strong smell drifted on the wind. I quickly took a few steps back and turned away.

Two sets of headlights were approaching us. As they moved in to park nearby, I could see one was a police cruiser, and the other one was the ME's white van.

The cruiser's front doors opened and Talia jumped from the passenger's seat, tripping as she ran towards us. She wore the same flannel pajamas as when I'd first met her, and her hair was a tangled mess down her back. She almost glowed in the moonlight, her skin was so pale and waxy. Everyone parted to give her a path Ginger.

Not acknowledging any of us, she collapsed in front of the wire crate, sobs of relief echoing in the stillness.

Ginger finally moved. She popped up onto her stubby legs, her tail wagging fiercely, beating the sides of the crate. A sharp, happy *yip!* came from her.

"Oh, Ginger," Talia whispered. All the grief and hope and pain she'd been through evident in those two simple words.

I bent down to help her as her shaking hands fumbled with the clips to open the cage. Ginger scratched at them from the inside now, whining, impatient to be released.

"Here, let me." I popped the three clips opened and then grabbed Buddha's collar and backed up, giving them space.

"Thank you." Talia smiled up at me, her eyes shining.

And then Ginger flung open the door and was on top on Talia, knocking her over and licking her face madly. Tiny whimpers were mingled with soft laughter. I glanced around. Everyone was smiling. I bet they never got to see this kind of joy at a murder scene.

Buddha pulled from my grip and leapt over to sniff at Ginger, his whole butt wriggling. I gave him a few seconds, and then got him back under control.

"Are you ready to go home?" Talia whispered, as she held Ginger's furry face in her hands.

Ginger licked her chin. Her whole body vibrated with excitement.

Talia was radient as she looked up at me. "Elle, can you give us a ride?"

I cringed as I thought about Talia riding in my little rust bucket. But, I couldn't say no. "Sure."

As she stood, her gaze caught on the cab of the truck. The ME had opened both doors. Her eyes blazed as her face stilled. "That's him? The man who took Diggs away from us? And stole my Ginger?"

"Looks like it." Salma stepped into her line of sight. "You really shouldn't focus on him, though. That kind of anger can change a person."

Talia nodded. "You're right. All that matters now is Ginger's safe. Thank you, Detective."

I turned to Devon. He had his hands shoved in his jean's pockets, watching everything unfold. "See you back at... the bungalow?" "Home" seemed too presumptuous.

He nodded once. That was good enough for me.

I tried to roll my window up, but it was busted. Buddha must've broken it when he pushed it down to make his great escape. "You little bugger." Sighing, I cranked the engine, praying it would catch. It did, filling the car with exhaust fumes.

Talia sat next to me with Ginger panting happily on her lap. "Does this car have sentimental value to you, Elle?"

"Not really." I cast one last glance at the crime scene as I steered us out of the parking lot. "Why?"

"Oh, just wondering." She kissed Ginger between the ears.

I smirked. "Wondering why anyone would drive such a rust bucket?"

Talia laughed easily, the joy back in her spirit. "Well, I wouldn't have put it that way but yes."

Reaching back, I pushed on Buddha's chest. "Stop breathing on Talia," I admonished. "You drive what you have, I guess."

I pulled around Talia's circle drive and scratched Ginger softly under the chin. Her eyes twinkled, too, but she did look a bit thinner than the last time I saw her. "I can't believe she's really here."

"I can't either. It still feels like a dream." A beaming Talia hugged me tight. "I can't thank you enough for helping me get her back, Elle. I'm going to throw a dinner party for you and all your friends, so we can celebrate together. I'll call you."

Buddha pushed his face between the seats as Talia opened the car door. She patted his head. "Of course, you can come, too, Romeo."

I waited until they got safely inside and then made my way back to the bungalow, anxious to talk to Devon.

When we got there, he wasn't home yet. But I did notice the Christmas decorations didn't make me feel so bad now.

I went in and checked on Mom, who was sleeping. Then I decided it couldn't hurt to create a little romantic atmosphere. I quickly opened a bottle of red wine and threw together a plate of cheese and crackers.

The air held a chill, but it was still nice enough to sit outside. I arranged the food and glasses on the patio table outside and lit some candles. Then I sat out there, sipping on a glass of wine and watching the dogs play in the yard. Anxiously, I kept checking my phone in case he'd changed his mind.

I got a text from Sunny asking to set up a private doga session which, after a back and forth schedule check, we made for Thursday, two nights from now. I might need the money if Devon asked me to move out.

While I waited, I called Hope and told her everything that'd happened tonight.

"What are you wearing?" Hope asked.

I glanced down at my yoga pants and gray sweatshirt with the words "I don't need therapy, all I need is yoga" on it. Which was a flat out lie. "Does it matter?"

"Yes, of course it matters. Go put on something besides yoga pants. Something sexy."

I laughed. She knew me too well.

The dogs suddenly stopped playing and were looking into the house with alert expressions and wagging tails. "Too late. I have to go. He's home." After some final encouraging words from her, I hung up. Glancing up at the stars twinkling in the velvety sky, I said a little prayer that this wouldn't be our last night together.

Devon came through the opened slider and walked over to me. He looked really beat, with dark circles under his eyes and a shadow of stubble on his face.

I waved awkwardly. "Hi."

"Hi." He took in the table with an unreadable expression. Then he sat down and sighed.

The dogs ran over, sniffing him excitedly. With his head bent, he rubbed both of them under the ears.

I watched him silently, my back stiff, anxiety starting to creep in. Would he tell me it's over? Ask me to leave now?

"Go on, go play." He shooed the dogs back into the yard and turned his attention to me. "Long day." Then he picked up his wineglass and took a swallow. "Hits the spot, thanks."

I relaxed a little under his soft tone. The anger seemed to have dissipated. "Oh, before I forget, last night the dogs were barking around two in the morning. I didn't think anything of it, until this morning when I found a note at the front door. It said stop interfering or the dog dies." I watched Devon's protective instincts rise with the heat in his face. "But the threat is over now, anyway," I quickly added.

His jaw twitched and his eyes blazed dangerously. "I shouldn't have left you alone."

I reached over and grabbed his hand. "I was fine. But Salma did say you should put up some security cameras."

He nodded and took a deep breath in through his nose.

I released his hand reluctantly and then sat back in my chair. Time to change the subject. "Did the ME confirm Leo had a heart attack?"

He shook his head, stretching out his legs and crossing one ankle over the other. "Actually he thinks the poor fella was poisoned."

I blinked. "Poisoned?"

He twisted his glass thoughtfully on the table. "There was some vomiting, a strange rash... some things that made him suspicious that, if it was a heart attack, it was caused by somethin' else."

How awful. "If that's true, then Leo definitely wasn't acting alone. Would Eva or Georgy be cold enough to poison a member of their own family?" I thought about how they both treated him at the HOA Christmas party. Not very kindly.

"Salma's betting on Eva, since the Moon Key Gazette was used for the photo of Ginger, which probably meant she was being held on the island. Salma's getting a search warrant. See if they can't come up with any of Ginger's hairs or saliva at Eva's place. That would at least prove she was involved."

I would've put my money on Georgy. But I guess Salma's been at this a long time. She'd have better instincts than me.

Buddha trotted up and squished a slimy rubber ball against my leg. "Drop it." I picked it up with two fingers and chucked it into the yard, watching him bounce after it. Then I thought of something. "Remember when we were at Sunny's house? I noticed a boathouse out back. Maybe Eva has one, too? That would be the perfect place for her to hide a dog."

Devon nodded. "I'll text Salma now and make sure the boathouse is included in the warrant." When he was done, he tossed his phone on the table and leaned forward, taking my hand in his. "Look, Elle, I don't feel well that we're on the outs like this. I know you did what you did for me. It's my problem to deal with, this jealousy, not yours. I want you to know that. It bothers me more that you didn't feel you could come to me with your plan beforehand. But that's on me, too."

I was shaking my head, holding onto his hand for dear life. "I shouldn't have gone behind your back." I choked on the relief flooding through me. "I'm so sorry."

He lifted my hand to his mouth and pressed his warm lips against my knuckles. "You have nothin' to be sorry for."

We spent the next few hours under the stars, catching up and easing back into a comfortable place with each other. I got a text from Talia around midnight and we used that as a signal it was time to go to bed.

I read it and then said, "Dinner party tomorrow night, Talia's place. To thank us for all our help getting Ginger back."

Devon draped his arm across my shoulder and I had the strangest sensation of being home. "I can say this now. I really didn't think she'd be gettin' that dog back. It's a bloody miracle."

I slid my arm around his waist. "Me either. I just hope Eva Gold doesn't get away with murder."

TWENTY-ONE

After my second class was over Wednesday, I drove back to the bungalow. I was a bit more excited than I should've been. It was time to take Mom back to her own house, and I felt like a heavy weight was being lifted off my chest. I'd deal with the guilt later with my therapist.

She was sitting on the edge of the bed, clutching her bag of belongings when I got there.

"You get all your medication?" I asked.

"Yeah. Bet you'll be glad to finally get rid of me," she grumbled, as I tried to help her up. She smacked my hand away. "Nothing wrong with my legs."

I gritted my teeth. "Want anything to eat for the road?"

She waved her hand behind her as she waddled unsteadily out the door. "Don't bother yourself."

I got her situated into the cramped front seat of my Beetle, while Buddha sat in the back, panting.

"That dog gonna breathe all over me the whole trip?" she asked, giving Buddha a side-ways glare.

"Buddha, get back," I said, pressing his chest so he sat back more in the seat. I really needed to tighten his harness. "Better?"

She grunted and stared out her side window. "This window's got dog slobber all over it. Can't even barely see out."

I rolled my eyes, a harsh grinding noise filling the air as I shoved the gearshift in reverse and backed out of the driveway.

Just twenty minutes. You can do it.

She didn't speak again until we'd driven off the private ferry and were sitting in traffic on Memorial Causeway, my car vibrating roughly around us. I really needed to get it in the shop. Why was life so much maintenance?

"This car feels like it's gonna fall apart around our ears. How come your fancy, rich boyfriend doesn't get you a new one?"

I pushed my sunglasses up on my nose and glanced over at her. "Why should it be his responsibility to buy me a car? And how do you know Devon has money anyway?"

She shrugged a meaty shoulder. "People talk. And if he really loved you, he wouldn't want you driving around in this piece of crap. I'm sure it's an embarrassment to him anyway."

"Devon's not like that." I bit the inside of my lip.

Was that why she'd been so uncharacteristically nice to Devon that day I'd brought him to meet her? Because she knew he had money? My face flushed with anger. Anger which gave me the courage to ask her about my father, who she'd refused to tell me anything about, except he'd left her when he'd found out about me. "Did Barry Allen ever buy you a car?" I heard the tremor in my voice. I hoped she didn't. Sometimes I thought she enjoyed getting me all emotional.

Her head whipped around and I felt her stare like hot coals on the side of my face. "Don't you get smart with me, Elvis. You know that man never gave me nothin' but you."

"Yeah, a worthless child." I whispered it under my breath, but I knew she'd heard me. I could tell by the way her shoulders stiffened and her chin rose.

She turned and stared out the window for the rest of the drive. I could feel her sulking.

It wasn't until I'd dropped her off at her cracker-box house with the fried brown grass, and then silently pulled away, that I let myself cry.

How could the woman who brought me into this world make me feel so worthless in such a short amount of time?

Buddha was back in his rightful spot in the front seat. He began sniffing the side of my face and then licked at the tears.

"Yeah, at least I have you. Good boy." I pulled his big, blocky head against mine. A string of saliva from his tongue dripped down onto my leg, but I didn't care. Love was messy.

Before I hit Memorial Causeway, I pulled over into a gas station. "Stay," I said, as I hopped out to fill up the tank. As I stood there watching the traffic go by, I thought about Leo. That poor kid. I knew I shouldn't feel sorry for a killer, but something had to go really wrong in his life for him to end up like he did. Was that "something" his father? Did he inherit the genes of a psychopath? That thought made me shudder. But one thing I'd learned is not to underestimate people when they get cornered.

When I'd finished pumping gas, I slid back into the squeaky, torn seat and checked the time. I still had an hour and a half before my four o'clock doga class. Enough time to check out Georgy's house and see if he owned a blue and white Bowrider.

"Up for a little adventure, Buddha?"

I got a lick on the ear, which I took for a *yes*. Such an agreeable dog.

You gotta love the internet. It took about ten seconds to find Georgy's address and plug it into Google maps. An eight minute hop onto the Causeway to Clearwater Beach. Perfect.

I hooked a right on Island Way, a thin strip of road between Clearwater Harbor and the Pinellas County Aquatic Perserve. All the houses here were waterfront, and most likely belonged to boat owners. Buddha had his head out the window, tongue flapping in the breeze. He barked once at a squirrel. If only humans were so easily entertained.

"Turn left in five hundred feet. Your destination will be on the right," the robotic lady in my phone told me.

I turned left into a cul-de-sac and found Georgy's house number on a two-story house with a red, barrel-tile roof and a brick driveway. It didn't look like anyone was home. I pulled up alongside the grass and shut off the engine. Maybe I should've left it running.

Oh well, too late. Here goes nothing. One thing I'd learned from Devon was just act like you belong somewhere and no one will question if you do. I went around to the passenger's side and opened the door. "Come on, boy. Let's go for a walk."

As we made our way through the side yard, between the houses, my pulse picked up speed. Feeling paranoid, I glanced behind me to make sure Angel wasn't there. She wasn't.

We strolled around a large, two-story lanai cage with a pool and spa nestled inside. And there it was. Floating in the canal under a wooden roof was the blue and white Bowrider.

I stopped for a second, glancing around. No movement so I pushed my trembling legs forward until we were standing in front of the boat. "I can't believe it. Think we really found the boat, boy." I snapped a few pics of it with my cell phone.

"Can I help you?" A woman's voice called from behind me.

I whirled around. A blonde woman in a blue maxi dress, her arms crossed, was staring at me from the screen door of the lanai.

"Oh," I said, shoving my phone back in my pocket, my heart now in my throat. I looked down and grabbed Buddha's collar. "No." I let out a fake laugh. "I got him. My dog. He just took off." I pulled Buddha with me as I headed back toward the side yard. "I got him. Thanks." Glancing down I saw the curious look Buddha was giving me, like, "Yeah, Mom, I know how to walk on my own, why are you pulling me?"

The woman didn't move. She just watched us until we disappeared back around the corner.

After I thanked the universe when my car started, we drove out of the cul-de-sac in a puff of gray smoke.

"Do you think she saw our car?" I was talking out loud, but Buddha was listening, so it didn't really count as talking to myself. "Yeah, she probably did. Does Georgy know what I drive? Was that woman suspicious enough she'd even mention my little visit to Georgy?" Well, only time would tell. For now, I had to get these photos of the boat to Salma. It proved Georgy was involved or at least his boat had been.

TWENTY-TWO

That evening we went to Talia's for the dinner party. I pushed aside my worries about Georgy's boat and if he'd find out about my visit. Salma said they'd look into it so it was out of my hands.

Besides, a new gratefulness was blooming in me as we gathered around Talia's table. I had so much love for these people, my heart was practically bursting. The way we'd all come together to help find Ginger. I felt like I'd finally found my place in this world. They say you can't pick your family, but I don't believe that anymore. These people felt like family to me.

Ginger was under the table, a white ball of fur curled up at Talia's feet. Talia said she hadn't left her side. Ginger had even greeted us at the door with Talia. Though she'd given me her squeaky frog and as I stroked it and told her what a beautiful baby it was, she'd cocked her head and woofed at me.

Talia had laughed then and said, "It's okay, Elle, she's done with her false pregnancy. It's a toy again."

So, I'd chucked it across the tile floor and was happy to see her scurry to retrieve it, tail wagging.

Buddha lay under the table, too, sprawled out between Ginger and my feet. I'd toed off my shoes and rested my bare feet on his back.

Talia raised her glass of champagne. Tonight, she looked like the Talia Hill we all knew from the movie screen, wearing a gold mini-dress and makeup, her flaxen hair fixed in a complicated up-do, her smile radiant. "I'd like to make a toast."

We all quieted down and smiled expectantly at our hostess.

"To you brave, selfless people who helped bring my Ginger back home. I am eternally grateful."

"Cheers," we all said, clinking glasses around the table.

"And to Ginger," Hope added. "And Holly, who I'm sure is smiling down at us right now, glad her sister is home where she belongs."

Talia's eyes were a glassy, bright blue as she gave Hope a loving smile and clinked her glass. "Thank you. I'm sure you're right."

Marcel brought in a large silver plate of appetizers and winked at me. "*Bon appetite.*"

As we each helped ourselves to the shrimp, stuffed mushrooms, and other offerings, Beth Anne asked, "Hey, Devon, is there any news on the investigation into Eva Gold? Have they searched her house yet?"

Devon swallowed and then shook his head. "Not yet. Still working on the warrant."

"The police really think Eva Gold was involved and poisoned her own nephew?" Talia asked, as she added some tiny pickles to her plate.

I nodded, scratching Buddha with my toes. "That's one theory. Though, I didn't get a chance to tell you guys. I went to her brother, Georgy's, house today and he has a blue and white Bowrider there, just like the one used in the first ransom hand-off debacle."

"Really?" Talia sat up straighter. "So, he may have been in on it with his son? Though, that would mean he poisoned his own son. Doesn't seem likely, does it? Are the police looking into it?"

"I hope he didn't do it. But yeah," I said. "I sent Salma... Detective Vargas some photos of the boat."

"Lord, if he did it... poisoned his own son. I mean, that's pretty hard core," Beth Anne said, her face stricken with horror.

"Being poisoned by his aunt is almost as bad," Devon said.

Lulu stabbed a coconut-crusted shrimp, shaking her head. "I can't believe I actually thought Leo Gold was cute. Am I destined to be attracted to violent men?"

I winced as I thought about how I'd almost set her up with him. I'd have to make sure I ditched that phone number and never mentioned it. "Devon will do a thorough background check on the next guy you date, don't worry," I teased.

She waved her fork. "No more men for me. Unless this baby is male. Then he'll be the man in my life."

"I'm sure you'll be too busy to date anyway. Word is already getting out around the island about your amazing menu at Café Belle, Lulu, congratulations," Beth Anne said, beaming a dimpled smile at her.

Lulu was glowing. "Thank you kindly. You know I never thought I'd like working in someone else's kitchen but Chef Pierre is a gem, and I'm learning so much from him. It's a good situation for now. Less responsibility and pressure for sure."

"Speaking of that." Talia rang a tiny bell and Marcel entered with a sly smile and a large, gold shopping bag. He handed it over to Talia. She grinned at us with a new flush to her cheeks. "I wanted to thank each of you for your kindness in caring about Ginger. I don't know you all very well, but I tried to make each thank you gift something special, and I will be offended if you don't accept it." We all shared a curious look as she dug into the bag and handed Lulu a gold envelope.

Lulu looked embarrassed as she accepted it. "Talia, you really shouldn't have."

Talia shrugged playfully. "But I did, so open it."

Lulu glanced around and then tore open the envelope. As she read, her eyes widened and then grew damp. "I can't." She was shaking her head, her spiral curls swaying, but her eyes stayed glued to the paper. "I can't accept this, Talia. It's too much."

"Nonsense." She waved her off. "Like I said, I'll be offended if you don't accept it."

"But Wallace & Hersh. They are the best of the best..." she was still struggling. She looked at me, her eyes panicked and handed me the paper. I read:

Wallace and Hersh will be handling your lawsuit over the restaurant now. All expenses paid. They will get your restaurant back. Their contact information was listed.

Tears sprang to my eyes, too. I glanced up at Talia and saw nothing but determination and affection. Then I handed the paper back to Lulu. "Let her help you. She wants to."

Lulu sprung out of her seat and hugged Talia. "Thank you," she whispered.

"You're very welcome. I've known them for years. They never lose." A happy Talia pulled the next gifts out of the bag as Lulu floated back to her seat, one hand cradling her belly.

Hope and Beth Anne squealed like school girls as they each held two tickets to a private red carpet celebrity event. "Oh, Talia... how fun! This is fantastic. Thank you!" they gushed.

"Devon Burke," she cocked her head. "You were the hardest. What to give a man that seems to have everything he needs?"

Devon glanced at me and threaded his fingers through mine. With a smile that could charm a snake, he said, "I do indeed have everything I need."

"Well, please accept this anyway." She handed him his own envelope.

He opened it and read it. Then read it again. "Is this for real?"

"Sure," she said, obviously pleased with his reaction. "He's a friend of mine. He's done headshots for me."

"What is it?" I leaned closer, trying to read the note.

"Only a private dinner invite with the most incredible photographer of our decade, Bowen Jay Jones. The man's a bloody genius. Old school. No post processing." He seemed years younger suddenly, the weight of his parents' murders, for that moment, lifting from his shoulders. "How did you know?" he asked.

"What? That you were a photographer before a private investigator? The internet, of course." She laughed. "Now... for you, Elle. I'm afraid you are going to have to wait until after dinner for your gift." She rang the bell again. When Marcel appeared, she said, "Have them bring in dinner, please."

It was a typical Christmas dinner American-style with honey-glazed ham and turkey, stuffing, sweet potatoes, mashed potatoes and gravy, five different types of roasted vegetables and salads. In the end, we were all stuffed and warmed by red wine, conversation, laughter and gratitude.

After Talia tried to stuff us more with an apple pie, which made everyone but Lulu groan, I glanced at the time. "We really should be heading home," I said reluctantly. "Petey probably needs to go out by now. This was an amazing evening in every way, though. Thank you, Talia."

She led us to the door, Ginger following her like a white shadow. Instead of stopping at the threshold, though, she continued outside to the driveway.

"And this, Elle," she said, "is your gift."

Stunned, I stood there staring at a shiny new, pale green VW convertible Beetle with a large red bow, letting her words sink in. It was the cutest car I'd ever seen. It looked like it had a glossy, cotton candy shell. My head was the first body part to move. I shook it as the girls squealed and went to check it out. "No, Talia, I can't accept that. It's too much."

She wasn't listening. She opened the passenger door and laughed as Buddha jumped in. "Someone likes it."

I finally got my feet to move. "Buddha get down," I said, approaching the little convertible. When he just stared at me with that squinty-eyed, tongue-hanging happy expression, I folded my arms. "Traitor."

Devon came up behind me and rubbed my lower back. He knew the struggle I had with accepting any help or gifts from anyone. He whispered in my ear, "Like you told Lulu, accept it. She wants to help."

Hope and Beth Anne were now gushing over the inside of the car. "Look, it has a little flower vase!" Hope called from the driver's seat.

Talia came over and gave me a stern look. "Elle, you were instrumental in getting Ginger back. This is the least I can do. Please accept it. I can't have a friend, who helped get me through one of the worst times in my life, drive around in a smelly, noisy car."

I felt myself softening. "I don't deserve this, Talia. I didn't do anything to deserve this and really, you don't owe me anything."

Talia threw her hands up. "It's just a car, Elle. It's not like I'm giving you an Oscar." She put her hands on her hips and a gleam appeared in her eye. "If you don't accept this, I'll take it back and buy you a Mercedes. And if you don't accept that, you'll wake up one day with a Lamborghini in your drive." She held up the keys, letting them dangle in front of me. "You don't know how stubborn I can be."

Feeling my shoulders fall, I finally smiled. "I'm starting to get the picture." I held out my hand. "Fine. Thank you but really, you shouldn't have."

"But I did, so get your butt in that driver's seat and start her up."

I breathed in the new car smell as I slid into the leather seat. The engine purred instead of coughed. The top slid smoothly back with a touch of a button. I could get used to this.

"Green is definitely your color." Talia leaned down and gave me a hug. "You do deserve it. But you can throw in a private lesson for Ginger if it will make you feel better."

Buddha barked excitedly.

We laughed. "I think he just said it would please both of us."

TWENTY-THREE

It was the first day I found myself relaxed enough to enjoy the Christmas decorations on the island. The fifteen-foot Christmas tree in the lobby of the Pampered Pup no longer felt like a giant pine-splinter in my spirit. Everyone seemed to be in a great mood in the doga classes, though I may have been projecting.

I still needed to find Devon a present, since my idea of getting him testimony from Alex went all kinds of sideways. He seemed really pleased with his date with the famous photographer. Maybe I could get him a print from the guy. *What was his name?* I'd have find that envelope or ask Talia. We had a doga lesson planned for tomorrow night. Tonight was my lesson with Sunny and her pacifier-loving pooch.

"I still can't believe this is ours," I said to Buddha as I opened the car door. The new leather smell drifted out, mingling with the oily, parking garage smell. Adjusting the rear view mirror, I startled as I caught a glimpse of Angel.

Twisting around frantically, I swept my gaze over the backseat. Empty. She wasn't there. *Was that my imagination?* "Did you see Angel?" I said aloud.

Buddha just licked his lips, his eyes locked on mine.

A tiny current of anxiety ran through my holiday cheer. "Well, either way, I'll just be extra careful." I started the car, letting the purr of the engine calm me down. "Careful of what though? That's the question."

Devon was down on the beach with Petey when we got home. I walked down to join him. It was dusk so the water was dark, but the sound of it lapping at the sand soothed my jangled nerves.

Petey play-bowed in front of Buddha and they started a game of chase.

"Hey." Devon greeted me with a kiss. I didn't realize how cold my face was until I felt his warm lips. "Got some news."

I smoothed down his thick hair, blown wild from the wind. "Yeah?"

He slipped his hand in mine. "Eva Gold's dog groomer has contacted me. Says she's got some information about Leo's death. She's agreed to come to my office tonight. If what she says connects Eva to Leo's death, Salma can get an arrest warrant and bring Eva in, while they search her home."

I squeezed his hand. "That's great."

He leaned back and stared at me. "I know that look. What's wrong?"

How could I tell him there might be danger, without telling him about Angel's visits from beyond the grave? Her visit meant I had to be extra careful, so I'm glad he didn't ask me to be there tonight when he met this dog groomer. But, what if her visit meant *he* was going to be in danger? After all, it was Angel's visit last time that saved his life.

I couldn't believe I was about to say this, considering I knew Salma had feelings for Devon but, "Can't you get Salma to come to your office while you talk to this dog groomer? For back up?"

There was still enough light left that I could see the confusion surface in his eyes. "Afraid she'll attack me with a grooming brush?"

I released his hand and rubbed my arms vigorously. The western wind was picking up and dropping the temperature. "I'm serious."

He brushed my hair out of my face and studied me. "You're concerned?"

"Yes."

He stepped forward and took over rubbing my arms, then kissed the top of my head. "Salma isn't available tonight but I'll be fine."

Leaning into his chest, the frustration bubbled up. He wasn't taking my concern seriously, which meant he might not be as alert as he needed to be. "Just promise me you'll be on the lookout for anything... an ambush or her leading you into a trap." I tilted my head back and looked into his eyes so he could see I was dead serious. "Anything your intuition tells you isn't right, you get out of there. I mean, for all we know, Eva could be using this woman to get you alone."

He nodded but looked more like he was amused at my concern.

I narrowed my eyes. "I'm serious, Devon."

He watched me for a moment and then kissed the tip of my nose. "You're right. She'd most likely be more loyal to her employer than me. I'll be careful. Promise."

"Thank you." I checked my phone. "I've got to go. Private lesson with Sunny and Leona tonight."

"The dog with the pacifier? How will you ever keep a straight face?" He grinned.

"I'm a professional." I wrapped my arms around him. Not laughing at her dog was the least of my worries. "I'll text you as soon as I'm done and you better text back."

I had every intention of going to spy on his meeting with Eva's dog groomer and watch his back when I was finished, but I wasn't going to let him know that. I should get done just around the time of their meeting. That tiny jolt of apprehension ran through me again. Then again, maybe I should just stay away. I groaned. *What to do?* I stuck my fingers in my mouth and whistled. Buddha trotted over and stared expectantly at me. "Come on, Buddha. Time to work."

Sunny seemed very excited about our lesson and, to my relief, Valentino wasn't there. She moved the coffee table aside, and we spread our mats out. I had Buddha stretch in front of me to demonstrate, but it took Sunny a good ten minutes to get Fiona to cooperate. She wanted no part of sitting on the mat.

"It's fine, just let her come to you when she's ready," I said, when I saw Sunny getting frustrated. "Meanwhile we'll do some gentle twists. Put your right leg out straight, bend your left knee and cross it over your leg like this."

Now that Sunny wasn't trying to get Fiona to sit on the mat, the little dog actually trotted over and began to sniff it. Her long bangs were pinned back with a red barrette between her ears.

"Just ignore her for now, let her get used to the idea that you're on the floor." This was probably the first time she'd ever seen her owner on the floor.

As I straightened my own back, my muscles knotted and I had to back off the twist so I didn't injure myself. I couldn't relax. My mind was firmly planted on Devon and his safety. All the different scenarios were like bees buzzing around in my head. I imagined Eva bursting through his office door with a gun. Or what if it was Georgy? He was big enough to hurt Devon without a gun.

That's it. As I led Sunny through a last twist, I couldn't stand it. I had to go and make sure Devon was all right. I'm sure Sunny wouldn't care that I was cutting the lesson a few minutes short. Especially now that Leona was sitting on the mat, leaning her tiny body against Sunny's stretched out leg. That was progress.

"That's a good girl, Leona," I said softly. "Now, Sunny, give her some attention to let her know it's a good thing she's there with you."

Suddenly Angel materialized in front of the sofa. Buddha turned his head toward her and sniffed the air. I looked away, ignoring her. I'd already made up my mind and she wasn't going to stop me. Not my most mature or rational moment.

"All right," I said, hearing the tremble in my voice. I could act brave, but my body apparently knew better. "Let's do one last full body stretch and then we'll call the lesson a success."

After we rolled up our mats, Sunny scooped up Leona and held her in her arms, stroking her long fur. The dog looked bored. "Didn't she do good? Like a pro, right?"

Still distracted by trying not to look at Angel, I nodded. "You both did great." I slid my mat back into its bag, my mind already out the door. "We can keep Thursday evenings as a standing lesson if you like?"

Sunny set Leona on down on the sofa. "Sure, that will work fine for January but then I'm off to Vancouver."

I nodded. I forgot most Moon Key residents travel throughout the year. Must be nice to not be terrified of flying. Or leaving the general area. I was definitely going to work on that phobia. Spending my whole life in one small space of this huge planet was just not an option. Especially when I was in love with a man who was in love with exploring.

When I turned to say goodbye, I noticed Sunny was biting her bottom lip nervously. She looked so vulnerable at that moment, I was taken aback. "Elle, there's something else I'd like to discuss with you. Will you have a quick cup of tea with me?"

Something she wanted to discuss with me? I silently groaned. *No!* "Sure." I kicked myself as the word left my mouth. Why couldn't I just say no for once? I really needed to go check on Devon. *You're too weak, Elle.*

Her shoulders relaxed with relief. "Oh thank you. Come on." She scooped Leona back up off the sofa and motioned for me to follow her. "We'll have it in the kitchen. I'm alone today."

Buddha was close behind as I took a seat at the kitchen table. I glanced down. Angel reappeared next to my leg. She faded in and out. Her dark eyes were the most solid part of her. They were locked on me, pleading. I got the message. Drink fast and get the heck out of here. I felt the adrenaline coursing through my veins, jacking up my heartrate. "I really only have a minute, Sunny. I have another appointment."

"I understand." She stood at the counter pouring thin, amber tea into two china cups and then carried them over.

When she sat mine down, I noticed her hand was shaking. *Did I do too much with her today? Or is she that nervous about what she's about to tell me?*

"This will only take a moment. I just need your advice. Woman to well... younger woman."

Oh heavens, is this about Valentino? Does she want advice from me on her love life? I felt myself blush. My leg was shaking nervously under the table. I picked up the cup and took a sip of the warm tea. It tasted like flowers. Time pressed in on me like a physical wall.

"Go on," I said, hoping to hurry her along.

"As you know, I'm dating a much younger man," she began, looking at me from beneath short, pale lashes. "Some people don't approve but I really am in love with him. And he treats me so well."

I took another mouthful of tea, nodding. Maybe I should ask for sugar. No, just let her talk and get it out. I was having a hard time focusing on her words.

Is the dog groomer already at Devon's office? What if Eva and Georgy are in on it together and they're both there right now grilling him on what he knows.

Angel barked. It was a sharp bark that sounded like it was right by my ear. I jumped and glanced down at her. Her mouth was closed tight and she was shimmering like a mirage. Those eyes, though. Dark and pleading. A solid warning.

"Are you all right, Elle?" Sunny tilted her head, her face softening with concern.

"Just..." Time to get out of here. Angel was standing now, doing circles. Trying to jump. "I just really hate being late." Grabbing the tea, I downed the rest of it and stood. "I'm so sorry, Sunny. Thank you for the tea, but do you mind if we continue this conversation next time?"

She looked disappointed but quickly recovered. "No, of course not."

"Appreciate your understanding." Hurrying over, I set my cup in the sink next to two other cups half-filled with old coffee and a plastic dog dish.

Buddha grunted as he pushed himself off the ground, his attention shifting between me and Angel.

I shoved in the kitchen chair and tried not to glance back down at Angel, who was shimmering and dancing at my feet.

Sunny seemed embarrassed, but she did offer me a smile as she waved me off. "It's no big deal. You go. We'll have another session next week and we can talk then."

Heavens, I did feel bad. The poor woman was obviously feeling insecure and needed some girl talk. But Devon's life may be in danger. That trumped social etiquette. "Yes, next week, I promise."

My hands were shaking as I started my new car. Mostly because Angel was now fully materialized in the back seat, panting and pacing. "Hang on, Devon. I'm coming."

Should I call Salma? It would take her too long to get on the island, even if I could reach her. I could call Moon Key security. What would I even say? *My ghost dog is freaking out and I think Devon's in danger.* And if Alex responded, it would be his life in danger. I'm pretty sure Devon couldn't get the image of Alex with his hand on my hip out of his head.

The only thing to do was to get there and see what was happening. I mashed the gas pedal.

TWENTY-FOUR

The traffic on Moon Key Drive was heavy. No one was in a hurry except me.

"Come on, come on." I tapped my foot impatiently as I sat at yet another red light in front of Island Grocery, a sea of cars crammed in its little parking lot.

The island was aglow, every palm tree was lit up with twinkling white and green lights, businesses were outlined in more lights, even the security building was decorated. I thought about stopping in there and grabbing whoever was on duty, but again... what would I say?

It took a frustratingly long time to get through the traffic, but I finally pulled into a parking space at Devon's office, next to his Jeep. Glancing in the back seat, I was relieved to find it empty. Angel was gone. *Am I about to stop the danger?*

"Okay, Buddha, you got my back, right?" His ears perked up, and he stared at me intently, trying to figure out what the game was. I grabbed my bag from the backseat and pulled out the mace Devon had given me. "Let's go."

He let out a soft *woof!* The word "go" he understood.

I scanned the area as I tiptoed toward the door. Buddha kept pace beside me, his ears alert. There didn't seem to be any movement around, except the palm fronds in the wind and the cars crawling along the main road. I pressed my ear up to the door. All I could hear was Buddha's panting. I glanced down at him. "Shhh." He closed his mouth and tilted his head. I could faintly make out a voice. A woman's. *Was it Eva or her groomer?* My stomach clenched and rumbled. I slapped a hand on it. Not now.

Closing my eyes, I reached for the door knob. Time to be brave. Be quick.

One. Two. Three!

I burst through the door, the tension ripping an involuntary scream from my throat. "Freeze!" I held the mace out in my shaking hand.

There were a few seconds of very long silence as I took in the scene.

Buddha trotted over to Devon and rested his head on his lap.

"Elle? Everything all right?" Devon was glancing from my face to the mace in my hand.

Is it? Taking in the office, I saw there was no sign of Eva or Georgy. I dropped my arm, and then slowly moved it behind my back.

A small woman with dyed pink hair had leapt out of the chair in front of Devon's desk. Her hand covered her heart as she stared at me with wide eyes behind black-framed glasses.

"Yes." I tried for a laugh, but it stuck in my throat. My face burned. "Looks like everything is fine. Sorry to intrude."

Devon stood up slowly and motioned between me and the woman. "Britany, this is my girlfriend, Elle Pressley. Elle, this is Britany, Eva's dog groomer."

I held out my hand, forgetting about the mace. "Nice to meet you."

Britany took a few steps sideways, eyeing the canister and then made her move toward the door. "I... I have to go. Call me if you have any more questions."

"Oh, Britany!" Devon moved around his desk quickly, trying to stop her.

She pulled open the door and disappeared through it.

"Thank you... for your help," Devon's voice trailed off. He turned to me with a smirk and held his hands up helplessly.

I fell into the empty chair. "I'm sorry I chased her away."

He sat on the edge of his desk, arms crossed. I was reminded briefly of our first meeting, the instant attraction I'd felt for him. A sense of awe washed over me. I was a lucky girl.

His blue eyes sparkled in amusement. "What's going on?"

Slipping the mace into my pocket, I said, "I really thought you were in danger. That Eva or Georgy would ambush you tonight."

He tilted his head. "Why would you think that?"

I felt my face grow warm again, so I dropped chin. "Just a hunch."

Buddha came over and rested his big blocky head in my lap. He'd apparently finished investigating the trash can. I slipped my hands under his silky ears and massaged his head. The act helped me relax enough to meet Devon's gaze. "I'm really sorry. Did she tell you anything useful?"

Devon shrugged. "I'm not sure. What she told me is Eva's nephew, Leo Gold, had an affair with Sunny Spillman when he was seventeen." He stopped and let that sink in.

"What?" I cried, startling Buddha. "How does she even know that for sure?"

He rubbed the stubble on his jaw roughly. "One thing you have to understand about most rich folks, their help are like the lamp in the room. They don't censor their conversations around them. Last night, while Britany was bathing Peaches in her mobile van, Eva was on the front porch ranting to Georgy about what a complete eejit Leo was for stealin' Talia's dog. How she wasn't even sure she was going to attend his funeral. That's when Eva also brought up his affair with Sunny when he was seventeen."

I was mortified. Leo was her nephew. How could she talk about him like that when he'd just died? "Doesn't sound like she's too choked up about her nephew's death. I knew she was cold, but that's just…" I shook my head as something dark and greasy churned my stomach. "So Beth Anne was right and Leo was the underage boy. That means Eva was using her own nephew to blackmail Sunny."

I recalled the conversation I'd overhead between Eva, Leo and Georgy at the Christmas party. Leo said Sunny had told him what Eva did. He must've been referring to Eva blackmailing Sunny about the underage affair. "Well, as shocking as that is, it still doesn't connect Eva to Diggs's murder or Ginger's dognapping."

Devon tented his fingers under his chin. "Let's say Eva wanted Talia's statue gone and took the matter into her own hands. She gets Leo to agree to do it somehow... maybe she blackmails him like she blackmailed Sunny."

I stood up and began to pace the office. "Eva did tell Georgy she did it for him. For all the hard work he put into the island Christmas lights. Most likely she was talking about smashing the statue, right?"

"Maybe. But she also could've been referring to blackmailing Sunny, to make sure Georgy kept the decorating contract." He rubbed his eyes and then clapped his hands together. "Anyway, back to the crime scene. Leo is surprised by Diggs during the vandalism and cracks him on the skull with the hammer. Not really meaning to kill him..."

I stopped in front of Devon. "Just a reaction to getting surprised. Which makes sense, because he didn't really seem like the murderer type."

Devon shoved his hands in his pockets. "And Leo wasn't supposed to take Ginger. That's not what his aunt told him to do."

"Or his father," I interjected.

"Right. But either way, Ginger's right in front of him, and he sees an opportunity to make some money..."

I nodded. "Yeah, that's the theory that makes the most sense to me. Money would motivate him, since his dad had him working the business from the bottom up, and he wasn't happy about it."

"It had to be Eva." Devon seemed to be getting excited, too. "Think about it. It had to be Eva's house he took Ginger to. It'd be too risky to try and take her off Moon Key to his da's, someone might remember. But Eva probably wasn't happy about him bringing the dog there, since it wasn't part of her plan."

"What could she say though, since she sent him to Talia's in the first place? She'd be an accessory to Diggs's death if he got caught with Ginger."

"Right," Devon agreed. "Eva has to give her maid vacation time, get her out of the house so they can hide Ginger. Leo stashes her there until he can get the ransom money. Then Eva decides to poison Leo while he has possession of Ginger, so Leo takes the blame for everything and can't tell anyone she was involved."

I felt sick and needed to sit down. "Which brings us back to the question, would she be cold enough to poison her own nephew?"

Devon walked around and picked up his cell phone and keys off the desk. "Well, Leo's autopsy was scheduled for today, and they're supposed to search Eva's house tomorrow mornin'. If Leo was indeed poisoned, and they can tell what kind of poison was used, they can look for it during the search. Salma's lettin' me be present during the search, so I'll fill her in on my conversation with Britney then."

"I hope they can find something on Eva. She can't get away with poisoning her own nephew." I was suddenly exhausted, and a dull headache was forming behind my eyes. Apparently I looked as tired as I felt.

Devon came over and helped me from the chair. "It's been a long day. Let's head home."

TWENTY-FIVE

A sharp stab of pain woke me up. I peeled my eyes opened, disorientated, and clutched my stomach.

Buddha was pressed against my back. Petey was sprawled across my feet. At the sound of my moan, Buddha moved his head to my shoulder.

Struggling to get my feet out from underneath Petey, I rolled over and a wave of nausea hit me, making the room spin. *Oh God.* I felt Devon's side of the bed. It was cold. He'd already left. *What time was it?* I tried to sit up. Paused. Let the room stop spinning. Another spasm clutched my stomach. I had to get to the bathroom. *Great.* Perfect time to get the flu.

I managed to sit up.

Angel shimmered at the bottom of the bed. She held herself rigid.

"Hey, girl," I croaked. I smiled, remembering how she'd stayed in bed with me for two weeks in sixth grade, when I'd had that awful bout of flu then. We didn't have health insurance, so I'd just had to "tough it out" as Mom put it.

All three dogs followed me as I crawled to the bathroom. Thank heavens I made it to the toilet before my dinner reappeared. As I rested my head on the cold porcelain, breathing heavy, I also thanked the stars that

Devon wasn't here to see me like this. Though, it would've been nice to still have Mom's nurse here. Maybe she would know a home remedy to shorten the illness.

A pounding and a barking grew louder in my awareness. I opened my eyes, disorientated. Taking in the bathroom, I suddenly remembered crawling in here and getting sick. Angel was standing in the doorway, tail and ears erect. I was so cold. *What are the dogs barking at?* It all felt like a dream.

The pounding came again. Someone was at the door. I tried to push myself off the toilet. My heart was racing. My stomach clenched and a fit of dry heaves gripped me. Resting my chin on my hand, I glanced at Angel. She was hopping toward me. She wanted me to answer the door. It was important.

Okay, girl.

With immense effort, I pushed myself upright and held onto the sink as the room spun wildly. I kept my focus on Angel, moving a bit at a time, holding myself up by leaning against the bathroom wall and then the bedroom wall. Falling forward, I managed to make it to the kitchen bar and then pulled myself along each chair.

"Coming," I tried to say. My heart was skipping in my chest, and my vision was constricted to one small tunnel of light. This was the worst flu I'd ever had.

Something sharp and ugly was trying to push its way to the front of my mind. *What?* I kept my focus on Angel as she led me forward. The ugly thought was almost there.

Buddha and Petey were sitting in front of the door, still barking and wagging their tails.

I had to fight my lungs to pull in air. My ears were ringing. *Had the knocking stopped?*

I managed to crack the door open but everything felt so far away.

And then the ugly thought was suddenly there. It had arrived with an image… the plastic dog bowl in the sink. The memory was sharp and terrifying, and I knew exactly what it meant.

The ringing in my ears had become a roar. I blinked in confusion at the man standing in the doorway. "Alex?" I had to say it. Get it in the light. "Poisoned."

Then I fell forward into his arms.

TWENTY-SIX

I became aware of the beeping sound first. Fighting through the grogginess, I forced my eyes open. My stomach felt like someone had stomped all over it with lead shoes and my throat was on fire. Turning my stiff neck, I surveyed my surroundings. Tubes and wires were connected to me everywhere. But, I managed a smile. I was alive.

"Hi," I croaked.

Devon jumped out of the chair and fell onto the bed beside me. His eyes were shot through with red veins and glistening with unshed tears. "We've got to stop meeting like this."

"What happened?" I forced the words past the fire in my throat.

He poured me a glass of water and maneuvered the bed so I could sit up to sip it. "You solved the case, and it almost bloody well killed ya. Do you remember anything?"

I searched through my foggy memories.

I had woken up sick as a dog. The cold bathroom floor. The vomiting. The knocking. The struggle to answer the door. Angel. Alex. I glanced at Devon. "Alex?"

He nodded. "He got you to the hospital in time. You told him you'd been poisoned. If you hadn't figured that out, you might not be here now. The doctors were able to work fast with that information to save your life. When Alex called me, and told me what you'd said, we knew it had to be the same poison used to kill Leo... oleander made into a diffused tea. And the same person."

I tipped my head so I could see the foot of the bed. Angel was there, stretched out and looking very pleased with herself. She'd tried to warn me. If only she could speak. I would've been able to understand she was trying to tell me not to drink the tea. I silently thanked her.

Turning my attention back to Devon, I said, "Sunny Spillman. I didn't realize it was her until it was too late. I remembered the plastic dog bowl in her sink right before I passed out. There were two tiny ceramic bowls on the kitchen floor so the plastic bowl wasn't Leona's."

Devon squeezed my hand between his and nodded. "Leo had been paid to destroy the glass statue, but by Sunny, not Eva. Sunny was the one who'd confronted Talia about the statue in the first place, remember? When Talia didn't remove it, Sunny took it personally. In her mind, it had escalated into a feud."

"A feud? That'll be news to Talia." I would've laughed if it all wasn't so tragic. "So Diggs died because Sunny thought Talia was defying her personally? Way to make it all about you, Sunny." I winced as my stomach tightened and ached with the rush of anger. "People like her shouldn't have any power. Not even being on the board of an HOA."

Devon gently smoothed the hair off my forehead and then stroked my arm. "Agreed. And we were right. Snatching Ginger wasn't part of the plan. It was a crime of opportunity. Leo took Ginger to Sunny's house that night, not Eva's like we'd thought. The police found Ginger's fur and saliva in Sunny's boathouse, where they'd kept her."

I recalled standing in Sunny's livingroom, staring out the window at that boathouse. If only we'd known Ginger was in there. At least she was home now.

I was relaxing under Devon's touch. "So why poison Leo?"

"Because Sunny got spooked. She wasn't sure she could trust Leo to keep his mouth shut about it bein' her idea to destroy the statue. Plus she figured if Leo died in possession of Ginger, the police wouldn't look into it any further and would close the case."

"So, she poisonened Leo and made it look like he was trying to leave Moon Key with Ginger?

Devon nodded and entwined our fingers. His expression darkened. "And she poisoned you because of some conversation you'd had with her at the HOA Christmas party. Apparently she got the idea that you suspected she was involved."

I recalled my conversation with Sunny that night and cringed inwardly.

"She had asked me about a private lesson, right after I'd mentioned something about a board member being an accessory to murder, if they were involved in destroying the statue."

Note to self, bluffing is not a good idea. Especially when you don't know you're talking to a cold-blooded killer disguised as a dainty southern belle.

I shifted my sore body in the bed. Trying to put these pieces together was taxing my brain. "What about the boat? Was Georgy in on it, too?"

"He wasn't. Leo still lived at home and had access to his father's boat. Georgy is pretty devastated."

I did feel bad for him. I couldn't imagine losing a child. "And what about Sunny's boyfriend, Valentino? Did he know what she'd done?"

Devon shook his head. "Salma has interviewed him and doesn't think he knew. He seemed pretty shaken up."

I nodded, letting my eyes drift closed. Then I forced them open. "Oh, what about Alex? Why was he at the house?"

Devon smiled, which confused me because any mention of Alex would usually elicit a stormy expression.

"He dropped by because he wanted to let us know he'd thought about what you'd said and decided you were right. He doesn't want to be a coward. He's going to tell the police that his original statement stands, and he'll testify to the conversation in the bar that night. He actually apologized to me." He squeezed my hands. "You did that. There are no words, Elle. You've given me a bloody miracle. Between Alex's testimony and the GPS information we've found on that second boat used, we can nail those bastards."

I blinked, trying to see through the blur of happy tears. A miracle indeed. "Merry Christmas," I whispered.

Devon's eyes lit up. "Speaking of. You better get well quickly because your Christmas present won't open itself."

⸺⟡⸺

The following day there was a parade of visitors through my hospital room.

Lulu was happier than I'd ever seen her. Her face glowed as she told me how good it felt to be cooking again and how the law firm believed they could beat the lawsuit. She'd even placed my hand on her belly to feel the baby move. She was really getting excited about their future.

Hope was helping Beth Anne plan a huge baby shower for Lulu, months in advance, so I could only imagine how over-the-top it was going to be. I even got a visit from Talia in disguise, who'd made me promise we'd try another doga lesson with Ginger as soon as I felt up to it.

Angel disappeared after that first night. I dreamed of her, though. We were running on the beach, her nipping at my heels, until I fell and she covered my face with kisses. It felt so real. I woke up once and the scent of her damp fur still lingered in the air.

I had plenty of time to wonder how my life had become filled with all these magical women, one amazing guy and two dogs, whom I missed greatly. Gratitude seemed like too small a word.

⸺⟡⸺

I was discharged on Christmas Eve, which was also the evening of the boat parade. Devon and I skipped the parties we'd been invited to and instead planted two lawn chairs in the sand. Sharing a blanket under the stars, we talked and laughed as we waited for the decorated boats to make their appearance.

The dogs were stretched out happily at our feet. Actually, Buddha was lying directly on my feet, apparently letting me know I wasn't going anywhere without him again.

Devon pulled an envelope out of his jacket pocket and held it for a moment. Then he looked at me, his expression a mixture of excitement and apprehension. "I'm going to give you this. It's your Christmas present, but I also want to give you the option not to accept it. You won't hurt my feelings."

I pushed my hair out of my eyes, letting the breeze blow it back from my face. "What do you mean? Why wouldn't I accept it?" My heart skipped a beat. "Is it a trip?" I didn't think I was ready to take a trip yet. I was still working on my anxiety. *Oh no, what if it's a plane ticket?*

"Because." He licked his lips and took my hand under the blanket. His eyes held mine. "Because this is information on... well, I found your da, Elle. That's the secret case I've been working on these past few weeks."

I let my gaze drop from his face to the envelope in his hand. A mixture of fear, disbelief and curiosity welled up and froze my thoughts. *Do I want to meet my father?* The decision was much easier when that wasn't an option.

"Say something," Devon whispered. "Are you upset with me?"

I got my mouth to work. "No, of course not. It's an amazingly thoughtful gesture. I'm just... unsure. I'm still really angry with him. No, maybe angry isn't the right word. From what little my mom has told me about him, I'm not sure he's worth getting to know. And he obviously didn't want anything to do with me. I don't think I could take the rejection."

But, I found myself reaching for the envelope anyway. I held it, still sealed, as the first boat rounded the island and came into sight. It was a yacht outlined in gold twinkling lights; three animated reindeer were planted up front and a giant blow-up Santa sat on top.

"And it begins." I rested my cheek on Devon's shoulder.

Petey and Buddha suddenly stood up, ears alert. They were staring behind us, toward the bungalow.

I turned in my chair to see what had caught their attention and smiled.

Hope and Ira were making their way through the sand, beach chairs slung over their shoulders. The bungalow's Christmas lights were flashing now, in sync with the rest of Moon Key's lights and with the music being pumped over high watt speakers from the guest dock.

I remembered taking the boat tour with Hope and her dad back in tenth grade. It was one of my fondest memories. And now, here I was, on the other side of the poverty line. Life was strange.

"Hello!" Hope called, waving.

As they got closer, I noticed a small figure trotting along behind them.

"We're not intruding, are we?" she asked, eyeing our cozy blanket set-up.

"Not at all. Who's this?" I leaned over to pet the wiry-looking brown dog with bat ears. He sat down, his head low while Buddha and Petey sniffed him over like two Hoover vacuums. "Oh, he only has one eye. Poor baby," I said.

"This is Jack," Hope said, unfolding her chair and situating it in the sand next to mine. "As in one-eyed Jack."

Ira shook Devon's hand and then placed his chair on the other side of Hope's. "We decided that, while no dog could ever replace Jelly-Belly, we were ready to give another dog a chance at a better life. So, we went to the shelter today and said, give us your most un-adoptable dog. And they brought out this guy."

"Not the cutest dog in the world, but isn't he sweet?" Hope cooed.

"He really is." I stroked his large bat-ears. He perked up. "And such a good boy," I whispered to him. "Well, congratulations on your new baby. I thought you guys were going to Beth Anne's party?"

"We were but we didn't want to leave Jack alone the first night in his new home," Ira said. "You sure you guys don't mind us crashing your private party?"

"Not at all." Devon squeezed my leg affectionately under the blanket.

"Oh, look at that sailboat!" Hope pointed excitedly and clapped, just like she had when we were growing up.

"It looks like a floating Christmas tree. Now that was a lot of work."

As the dogs coaxed Jack into a game of chase on the beach, we watched the parade of boats float by under a quarter-moon. My foot tapped to the beat of music and I sighed in contentment. This was pure Christmas magic.

When the tour boats came, they turned the tide on us, and Moon Key was suddenly the spectacle, with air-horns being blown to show their appreciation. We could also hear the distant whistling and clapping floating on the evening breeze.

I decided I would just enjoy this moment, this night, and not make a decision yet about whether I wanted to meet my father.

Tomorrow was my first Christmas with Devon, and I wasn't going to let anything interfere with our happiness. I breathed in the chilled, salty air. A shooting star streaked across the dark sky. I made a wish. I wished that I could freeze time and stay as happy as I was at this moment. A girl can dream, can't she?

www.ingramcontent.com/pod-product-compliance
Lightning Source LLC
Chambersburg PA
CBHW021958170626
46808CB00001B/212